People chanted the numbers together. "Ten…nine…eight…"

"We could get hurt again," he said.

"Five…four…three…"

"Very hurt," she whispered, and her gaze locked on his. The heat that had been building between them reached a fever pitch. His gut tightened with desire, and he realized that the most magical thing in the room was Jenna.

"Two…one… Happy New Year!" Cheers erupted around them, horns blew, glasses clinked and the band launched into "Auld Lang Syne."

They were old acquaintances, just as the song said, and if they were really honest with each other, they'd admit the truth. They'd never forgotten, not for a moment. And right now all Stockton wanted to do was remember her, remember this.

"Happy New Year, Jenna," Stockton whispered, then he closed the gap between them and kissed her.

Dear Reader,

I hope you enjoy this return visit to Riverbend (which was featured in *Miracle on Christmas Eve* and *Marry-Me Christmas*)! I love writing about small towns. I grew up in one, and every time I go back home to visit my family and friends, it's like a reunion. I've lived in another state for more than a decade, yet, when I return to the place where I grew up, it feels as if I never left. There's just something about the comforting warmth of a small town that wraps around the people who live there now, and lived there before, like an old, soft blanket.

After writing two Christmas stories set in Riverbend, I thought it would be fun to choose another holiday. New Year's Eve is always a great one, not just because of the confetti and countdown, but because it's also a holiday that inspires new beginnings, hopes for a transformed future and limitless possibilities. I've had a few memorable New Year's Eves in my life (including one when I was stuck on a broken subway train in Boston at midnight, and all the passengers did the countdown together in the dark), and each year I look forward to that symbolic division between the old and the new.

I hope you enjoy Jenna and Stockton's story, and the town-wide New Year's Eve party in *Midnight Kiss, New Year Wish*. I had a lot of fun returning to Riverbend and hope to go back to the town again in future books. I always enjoy reader mail and email, so feel free to write to me at Shirley Jump, P.O. Box 5126, Fort Wayne, IN 46895, or visit my website at www.shirleyjump.com. And for some tried-and-true recipes for your holiday season (meaning my family has tried them and voiced their opinions!), visit my blog at www.shirleyjump.blogspot.com.

Have a wonderful New Year and thank you for reading!

Shirley

SHIRLEY JUMP
Midnight Kiss, New Year Wish

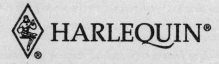

TORONTO • NEW YORK • LONDON
AMSTERDAM • PARIS • SYDNEY • HAMBURG
STOCKHOLM • ATHENS • TOKYO • MILAN • MADRID
PRAGUE • WARSAW • BUDAPEST • AUCKLAND

Recycling programs
for this product may
not exist in your area.

ISBN-13: 978-0-373-17705-9

MIDNIGHT KISS, NEW YEAR WISH

First North American Publication 2011

Copyright © 2011 by Shirley Kawa-Jump, LLC

New York Times bestselling author **Shirley Jump** didn't have the willpower to diet, nor the talent to master under-eye concealer, so she bowed out of a career in television and opted instead for a career where she could be paid to eat at her desk—writing. At first, seeking revenge on her children for their grocery-store tantrums, she sold embarrassing essays about them to anthologies. However, it wasn't enough to feed her growing addiction to writing funny. So she turned to the world of romance novels, where messes are (usually) cleaned up before The End. In the worlds Shirley gets to create and control, the children listen to their parents, the husbands always remember holidays and the housework is magically done by elves. Though she's thrilled to see her books in stores around the world, Shirley mostly writes because it gives her an excuse to avoid cleaning the toilets and helps feed her shoe habit. To learn more, visit her website at www.shirleyjump.com.

Praise for Shirley Jump

"Shirley Jump winds up A Bride for All Seasons with
Marry-Me Christmas, a sweet story with terrific characters
and a well-constructed plot."
—*RT Book Reviews*

About *Sweetheart Lost and Found*
"This tale of rekindled love is right on target:
a delightful start to this uplifting, marriage-oriented series
[The Wedding Planners]."
—*LibraryJournal.com*

About *New York Times* bestselling anthology *Sugar and Spice*
"Jump's office romance gives the collection a kick,
with fiery writing."
—*PublishersWeekly.com*

To the Stone Soup Sisters. For all the advice, laughs and hugs over the years. I couldn't pick a better or more diverse group of friends.

CHAPTER ONE

THICK, WET, HEAVY SNOW tumbled onto Jenna Pearson's shoulders, blanketing her black hair, and seeping into her black leather high-heeled boots, as if Mother Nature wanted to test Jenna's resolve. To see whether a winter storm could derail her plans, and force her back to New York.

Jenna kept forging forward. Really, what other choice did she have right now? If Jenna had one quality, it was that ability to rush forward, to keep going when it seemed like all was lost.

And right now, just about all was lost. But she had a plan, and she'd get it all back. Definitely.

A two-inch carpet of flakes covered the sidewalk as Jenna walked, under the swags of Christmas pine, past the crimson bows dotting the wrought iron lamp poles. Downtown Riverbend had already buttoned down for the night, with most of the specialty shops lining the street shuttered and dark. Only the café's windows glowed, like a beacon waiting at the far end of the white storm.

Jenna drew her coat tighter and dipped her chin to bury her nose in her blue cashmere scarf. She'd forgotten how cold winters got here. Forgot how the snow carried a fresh, crisp scent. Forgot what it was like to be in the small Indiana town that most people called heaven.

And Jenna had called prison.

The streets were empty, quiet, people safe at home and in bed. She was in Riverbend, after all, the kind of town where nothing bad ever happened.

Well, not nothing bad, but not *that* kind of bad. She was safe. Perfectly safe.

She increased her stride. Goodness, the snow seemed to have doubled in strength and depth in the twenty minutes it had taken her to buy a dozen cookies at the Joyful Creations Bakery. Even though she'd come in at closing time, the owner, Samantha MacGregor, had insisted on staying to fill Jenna's order—and then spending a few minutes over a cup of coffee catching up with her high school friend. Jenna had heard just about everything about everyone in town, even about people she wasn't so sure she wanted to be reminded of.

People like Stockton Grisham. He was here in town, Samantha said. "Returned a few years ago, and opened up a restaurant."

Stockton had returned to Riverbend? The last she'd known, he'd intended to wander the world, plying his culinary talents in some far-off location. He'd told her he wanted to make his mark on the world, one bouillabaisse at a time.

What was it about Riverbend that kept people coming back, or worse, encouraged them to never leave? Most days, Jenna was definitely happy she had left.

Or thought she had been. For so many years, New York had been the only destination she wanted, the only address she imagined for herself. And now...

She increased her pace, shushing that persistent whisper of questions she didn't want to face. The snow blew and swirled around her but she kept going, her boots crunching on the icy crust forming over the snow. As she walked, sharp notes of ginger wafted up to tease at Jenna's senses, tempting her to eat one—just one—of the homemade wind-mill cookies.

She got into her car, laid the box of cookies on the passenger's seat and turned the key, waiting while the wipers brushed off the coating of snow building up on the windshield. When the windshield was clear, Jenna put the auto into gear. The Taurus fishtailed a bit, protesting how quickly Jenna had pulled away from the curb. She pressed on the brakes. Took in a deep breath. It had been a long time since she'd driven in snow. In New York, she walked almost everywhere, cabbed or subwayed it for longer distances. Riverbend was no New York. There wasn't any public transportation or yellow taxis. Just her and the mounting snow—

And the job ahead of her.

She thought of turning back, of heading for the airport and retreating to her third-floor walk-up apartment in New York. Anything other than return to the town that had whispered about her life like it was an ongoing soap opera. She supposed, in many ways, it had been. But that had been years ago, and surely things were different now.

Jenna's hand hovered over the turning signal. Take a left? Or go straight?

Really, what was waiting for her if she turned left, and got back on that plane? Her only opportunities lay straight ahead, in this town she had tried so hard to leave behind, and now had become her only salvation. Riverbend, of all places. Jenna sighed and started driving.

Swags of evergreen hung across Main Street, connecting to big red bows adorning the streetlights. The streetlights glowed a soft yellow against the white snow. Jenna didn't pause to admire the view. Didn't slow as she passed the town's Winterfest decorations glittering in the park and still blinking a rainbow of colors even now, two days after

Christmas. She drove two blocks, took a right, then pulled to a stop in front of a big yellow farmhouse-style home with white wagon wheel trim decorating the expansive front porch. Fat low shrubs ringed the house, all of them twinkling with tiny white bulbs that peeked out of the snow with a determined glow.

Before Jenna reached the top step, the front door was flung open and her aunt Mabel came hurrying out the door, her house slippers padding across the dusting of snow on the porch, her bright pink robe flying out behind her like a cape. "Jenna!" She crushed her niece into a hug scented with cinnamon and fresh-baked bread.

Jenna's arms wrapped around Aunt Mabel's ample frame. It had been two years since she last saw her aunt, but as they embraced, and she took in her aunt's short gray curls and light blue eyes, all those months disappeared and it felt as if she'd never left Riverbend. If there was one blessing she'd received from this town, it was her aunt Mabel, who had done the most unselfish thing anyone could ask for, and raised her sister's child as her own. "I've missed you so much, Aunt Mabel."

Her aunt drew back and smiled. "Oh, honey, I missed you, too." Then she patted Jenna's hand and waved toward the house. "Now let's get on inside and I'll put on a pot of coffee. I know you're hankering for one of those windmill cookies you've got in your hands as much as I am."

Jenna laughed. "Am I that predictable?"

Aunt Mabel nodded. "And I love that you are." They went inside the house, warm air hitting Jenna with a burst. As Jenna glanced around, she realized very little had changed in the house she'd lived in most of her life. The same overstuffed crimson sofa set sat in the living room, the same pink striped wallpaper lined the bathroom walls and the same family portraits hugged the hallway. When she'd been a teenager, the day-in, day-out sameness had drove her crazy, but now, as a returning adult, familiarity bred comfort, and the tension that had seemed to hang on Jenna like a heavy blanket eased a bit.

A few minutes later, they sat down at Aunt Mabel's scarred maple table in her sunflower bright kitchen, two steaming cups of coffee and a platter of windmill cookies before them. Jenna picked up a cookie, dunked it in her coffee, then took a bite before the softened treat fell apart.

Aunt Mabel laughed. "You still do that."

"What?"

"Dunk your cookies. When you were a little girl, it was in hot cocoa. Now, it's coffee." Aunt Mabel's soft hand covered hers. "You're still the same."

The words chafed at Jenna, and she pushed her coffee aside. "I've changed. More than you know."

Aunt Mabel tut-tutted. "People don't change, honey. Not that much. You might think you do, but you always come right back to your roots. Why, look at you, you're here now. And just before the new year, too. There's no better time for a new beginning." She put up a hand. "Oh, wait. I think I still have some mince pie. You know you should have some in the days after Christmas, to bring good fortune for the year ahead."

"I'm fine, Aunt Mabel, really." Her aunt saw signs in everything from birds flying south to overly puffy clouds. Jenna wasn't in the mood to go down that portent-laden path. "I'm only back in Riverbend to plan Eunice Dresden's birthday party." Her gaze met her aunt's. "Thanks for recommending me."

Aunt Mabel waved off the gratitude. "That's what family's for, to give you a boost when you need it most."

Her aunt had no idea how much Jenna needed this boost.

She had no doubt it had taken some doing on her aunt's part to get the Dresden family to agree to hire her. "I appreciate it, all the same."

Aunt Mabel wagged a cookie at Jenna. "You stay here long enough, you might find this town growing on you again."

She loved her aunt, even if they had the same argument every time she'd seen her. The only thing she'd ever really loved about this small, confining town had been the warm and gracious aunt who had raised her after her parents died. From the minute Jenna realized a big, bright, busy world existed away from insular Riverbend, she'd wanted to leave. "It never grew on me. And I'm not staying. I already have a flight back booked for the night of Eunice's party. The party should be done by six, which means I can be on the nine-o'clock flight back to New York."

A nagging doubt grew inside her. Would this break from the city, from her faltering business, be enough to restore her? To give her back what she had lost?

Aunt Mabel pursed her lips as if she might say something else, but instead she got to her feet and refreshed her coffee. "Well, you're here now. We'll see about the rest."

"It's clear where I get my stubbornness from."

"Me? I'm not stubborn. Just…focused on getting what I want."

Jenna laughed. "Aunt Mabel, you should have gone into politics. You have quite a way of dancing around words."

The older woman returned to the table, and wrapped her hands around her snowman-decorated mug. "Are you going to see anyone special while you're in town?"

"Sorry to disappoint you, Aunt Mabel, but I'm here to work. Not visit with anyone." She put her hand out and grasped the older woman's fingers. "Except for you."

"Jenna—"

"I know you mean well, but really, I'm not going to have time for anything more than planning the party." Jenna got to her feet, put her mug into the dishwasher and gave her aunt a quick hug. "I'm going to bed. It's been a long day and I have the meeting with Eunice's family first thing in the morning."

"Good luck, sweetheart."

Jenna waved a dismissive hand, one filled with more confidence than she'd been feeling over the past few months. "Aunt Mabel, party planning is what I do. The whole thing will be a piece of cake," she said, telling herself as much as she did her aunt. She could do this—and she would. It was a birthday party, not a presidential dinner. "You'll see."

Aunt Mabel laughed. "You don't know Eunice's sister like I know her, honey. And you ain't met stubborn like her."

Delicious.

Stockton Grisham put the teaspoon into the deep stainless steel sink, then made a note on his clipboard to add the tomato basil tortellini soup to tonight's menu. It would pair well with the Chicken Marsala, and make a nice light side to the house's namesake Insalata Rustica. His restaurant was celebrating its first anniversary this week, an occasion that surprised even him sometimes.

He'd done it. Taken what had always been a dream and turned it into a living, breathing, forty-table reality. And what's more, made it work in the little town of Riverbend. Everyone—including his own father—had told him he was crazy, that no one from Indianapolis would make the trek to the "boondocks" just to eat dinner, but they'd been wrong.

He wasn't sure if it was the outdoor seating under the

canopy of ivy, or the cozy booths and cushioned chairs, or, he hoped, the authentic Italian food he made, but something drew people out of the city and into Riverbend for a night at cozy, intimate Rustica, followed by an hour or two of wandering Riverbend's downtown, a boon to the other local shops. It had become the perfect relationship, and a measure of pride swelled in Stockton's chest.

He'd done it. When he'd been young, he had never imagined returning to this town and being a success, but as he'd traveled the globe, it became clear that the only place he wanted to build his culinary career was here.

In the very town his father had thought lacked the sophistication to house a restaurant. To Hank Grisham, true culinary enjoyment could only be found in places like Paris, or Manhattan. Small towns, to his French-born father, were the antithesis of fine cuisine. Stockton's mother had loved Riverbend, and she'd stayed here, putting down roots, raising her son, while Hank traveled and cooked, taking a job here for a few months, there for another few. Stockton saw more postcards with Hank's signature than he ever saw Hank.

At some point, it had become a quest to prove his father wrong. To show him Riverbend could, indeed, house a top-tier restaurant and that the residents would fill the tables. Stockton sighed, and thought of Hank, manning a stove somewhere in Venice right now. One of these days, his father would come home to Riverbend again and see the restaurant in action. Maybe then the biggest naysayer of Stockton's dream would admit that there were more places than Italy to find amazing food.

Stockton had everything he'd always wanted. And yet, an emptiness gnawed at him sometimes, long after the dishes were done and the food put away, he wondered if there was...

More.

Insane thoughts. He had the more, and then some. He just needed to remember to count those blessings instead of looking for others.

The back door opened, and a whoosh of cold air burst into the kitchen. "Goodness, when is winter going to end?" Samantha MacGregor stomped the snow off her boots, then whisked a few flakes from her blond hair. Even bundled in a winter coat, Samantha was still beautiful. Her cheeks held a soft pink flush, and a smile seemed permanently etched on her face. Clearly, marriage agreed with her. Ever since reporter Flynn MacGregor had come to town a little over a year ago, Samantha had laughed and smiled almost daily. She'd had a hard time of it the past few years between her grandmother's illness and the full-time job of running the Joyful Creations Bakery. Stockton was glad to see his longtime friend find happiness.

"Considering it's not even January yet, I'd say we have some time before spring returns," Stockton said. "You have my cookies?"

She grinned as she undid a few of her coat's buttons with one hand. The heat of the kitchen sometimes hit like a wave, nice in the winter, not so much in the summer, even with the A/C running. "Of course. Though I had to get up early to run this batch. Between the publicity from that article Flynn did on the shop, and your constant orders, I'm about ready to start a third shift."

He chuckled. "Glad to hear business is good."

"I could say the same to you." She laid the boxes of fresh cookies on the counter. "So…how are you?"

"Fine." He grinned. "I know you're asking for a reason."

"Am I that transparent?" Samantha laughed. "It's just… well, I worry about you."

"I'm fine," he reiterated.

Samantha made a face. "That's not what Rachel said when she called me from her mother's house today. She said you were working yourself into the ground. She also said, and I quote, 'I see my manicurist more often than I see that workaholic.'"

He sighed. He took a taste of the marinara sauce simmering on the stove, then reached for the salt and pepper, and added a dash of each to the stockpot. A stir with the ladle, then another taste with a fresh teaspoon. Perfect. Too bad life couldn't be fixed as easily as a sauce. "Rachel and I disagree about my work schedule."

"You know," Samantha said, running a hand over one of the counters and avoiding Stockton's gaze, "one would say that a man who doesn't make a lot of effort isn't very interested in a woman."

Stockton cursed under his breath. That was the problem with having personal conversations with people who had known him nearly all his life—they were far too observant and far too vocal with their opinions. "Rachel and I were never really serious. In fact, I wouldn't even say we were much more than friends."

Samantha sighed. "Too bad, Stockton. Because I think you'd make someone a fabulous husband if you just reshuffled your priorities a little."

"I'm fine," he said for the third time, avoiding Samantha's inquisitive gaze by doing the whole tasting-stirring routine again.

Samantha turned to some bundled foil dishes on the countertop. "Are these ready to go?"

"Yep. There's a lasagna, a salad and a whole lot of bread. Thanks for making the delivery for me today. I wasn't sure when I'd find time, what with Larry calling in sick again today. I hate to disappoint Father Michael."

Samantha laid a hand atop the three tiers of leftovers. "The shelter really appreciates these donations, Stockton. Great food, cooked by a great chef, makes everyone feel better."

He shrugged. "Just doing my part, Sam."

"You do your part and then some." She began buttoning her bright red coat, her gaze on the fasteners, not on Stockton. That, he knew, meant she was about to say something he didn't want to hear. He'd been friends with Samantha most of his life and could read her as easily as the front page. "You know, I saw Jenna Pearson last night."

Good thing Stockton had stepped away from the stove, or something would have ended up burned. Instead, he stood in the center of his kitchen, a gaping idiot completely unprepared for those words. And pretending they didn't affect him at all.

It had been eight years since he'd seen her. Eight years since he'd walked out of her life. Afterward, he'd spent two years wandering Italy, learning Italian methods of cooking, but more, finding out who he was and what he wanted out of life.

This, he told himself, glancing around the expansive, gleaming kitchen, this was what he wanted. What he should focus his energy on—not a past that had returned to town. "Jenna Pearson back in town. Why?"

"She's here to plan Eunice's birthday party. The family hired her."

Had Jenna come all the way from New York for that one job? Or for something else? He told himself he didn't care. That he wasn't going to see her either way. Their relationship had crashed and burned a long time ago, a disaster ending worse than anything he'd ever done in the kitchen. "Is she, uh, going to stay for a while? Or leaving right after the party?"

"She's going back to New York right after the event."

"Well, if you see her, tell her I said hello." He didn't really mean it, but it seemed the polite thing to say. And being polite was his best course of action when it came to his ex-girlfriend.

"You should tell her yourself," Samantha said softly. "You know, you have that one-year anniversary coming up in a few days. Sure would help to have a party planner around to fine-tune things for you. Especially one you know as well as Jenna Pearson."

"Don't you have baking to do?"

Samantha grinned and tied the belt on her coat, then flipped up the collar. "Okay, I get the hint. I'll go back to my work, and let you go back to avoiding the obvious."

"And what's the obvious?"

She opened the door, but didn't step outside yet. "You're wondering how long you can hold out before you go see Jenna."

Jenna sat across from Betsy Williams, Eunice's younger sister and owner of Betsy's Bed and Breakfast, a veritable Riverbend institution. Jenna had known Betsy most of her life, and when she'd been little, had been just a little afraid of the stern older lady. Betsy was the kind of woman who kept her house in order, and expected everyone else to fall in line, too, whether they were just stopping by for trick-or-treating (ask right or there'd be nothing put in your pillowcase but air) or riding bikes along the sidewalk (leave room for the pedestrians and cut out those crazy handlebar tricks).

With her customers, though, Betsy was another woman. Effusive and welcoming, she embodied the bed and breakfast she ran in her buxom frame, quirky shoes and hats, and endless supply of food. The entire Victorian house was decked out for Christmas, with little elves hanging from the crown molding, dozens of kitschy Santas in every nook, bright reindeer-decorated towels and even a reindeer-head umbrella holder. Jenna heard Betsy had started dating Earl Klein last year. Jenna wondered if finding love with the irascible garage mechanic had softened Betsy.

If it had, that softening was nowhere to be found today.

"You know I only called you because your aunt practically strong-armed me into it." Betsy frowned.

Well. Betsy knew how to get right to the heart of the matter. Jenna swallowed. "I appreciate the opportunity—"

Betsy waved off Jenna's words. "Mabel says you're good at your job. I don't know about that. I am not impressed so far."

Jenna thought of the hours she had put into the party proposal. The time she'd spent trying to think of a unique menu, memorable centerpieces, quirky favors. She'd spent a half a day alone tracking down a vendor who could make a cake that would include a mechanical calliope in the center, one of the things Jenna had heard Eunice really enjoyed in her childhood. "I have lots of ideas that I think—"

"I know what you think." Betsy eyed Jenna. "You come in here, in your fancy New York clothes—"

At that, Jenna regretted choosing the Chanel suit and Jimmy Choo stilettos for the meeting. She'd thought the outfit would spell *successful, competent.* If anything, from that first step up the walkway in the designer shoes, she had probably alienated Betsy.

"—and think people like us need someone like you to show us what a good party is."

"I never said—"

"You left this town, and I think you forgot what it's like here. People around these parts don't want something like this," Betsy said, waving at the thick blue presentation folder emblazoned with the logo for Jenna's company, Extravagant Events. "Folks here aren't that fancy. I've been in the business of serving meals and making people happy for more than two decades, and one thing I learned long ago is that people come here because they like plain, simple food. That's what Riverbend is all about. *Plain and simple.*"

Jenna shifted in her seat. Had she really thought this would be easy? That she could come in here, and Betsy would welcome her with open arms? "Miss Williams, roasted Cornish game hens are simple."

"Maybe where you are, but not here." She shook her head. "If folks can't walk into the local SuperSaver and buy it, they sure as tooting aren't going to know what to do with it if they see it on their plate. Why, they'll say you've got pigeons on a plate." She pushed the folder back toward Jenna, then crossed her arms over her chest. "You'll have to serve something else."

"If you don't want the Cornish game hens, perhaps we could have a veal piccata or—"

"Do you know the only reason why the family decided to hire you?" Betsy didn't wait for an answer. She leaned forward, her light blue eyes sharp and direct. "It wasn't just because your aunt was blowing your horn. It was because you're a local and locals know what Riverbend folks like."

Jenna didn't bother mentioning that she had left Riverbend years ago. That she'd never felt like a local, not in all the years she'd lived in town. Even after she had moved from the farm and into that yellow house with Aunt Mabel when she was seven, she'd always felt caught between two worlds—the one that had been taken from her in an instant and the new one she was expected to adjust to as easily as a duck slipping into a pond. A world filled with whispers and innuendos.

She kept mum about the truth—that she wouldn't return to living here if it was the last town on earth. And that she'd only taken this job because she hoped for a glowing recommendation she could use to rebuild her business in New York. "I appreciate that, Miss Williams."

The front door opened and Earl Klein stepped inside, ushering in a blast of winter's cold with him. He shook the snow off his ball cap, wiped it from his jacket. "You wait right there, Earl Klein, and wipe your feet," Betsy said. "I won't have you tracking the outside in with those monstrous clodhoppers of yours."

Earl scowled, but did as Betsy ordered, going so far as to take off his boots and set them by the umbrella rack. He hung up his coat, then crossed to Betsy's side and pressed a loud, smacking kiss on her cheek.

She gasped and slapped him on the arm. "Earl!"

"And hello to you, too." He grinned, then plopped onto the sofa beside her, his lanky frame dwarfing the rose patterned loveseat. He took off his grease-stained "Earl's Garage" ball cap, went to set it on the coffee table, then saw Betsy's horrified glare, and dropped it on his lap instead. He ran a hand through his gray hair, making what was already a mess into a disaster. "Why, if it isn't Jenna Pearson," he said with a friendly grin directed Jenna's way. "Been a long time since you been back to this town."

"It has," Jenna said. At least someone was happy to see her.

"Well, we're glad you're here. Riverbend could use a blow-out bash," Earl said. "And I reckon you're the right one to do it."

Betsy harrumphed.

"Now, Miss Williams, back to the menu," Jenna said, opening the folder and pointing to the list of entrée options. "We could also try—"

"A hog roast," Earl cut in. "Get a big fat porker from Chuck Miller's farm. Slap that baby on a spit, stick an apple in its mouth and wham-bam, dinner is done."

"A hog roast?" Jenna repeated. Surely she'd heard him wrong. They couldn't possibly think a hog roast would be appropriate for an event like this. For one, how on earth would she get a spit and a several-hundred-pound pig into the hall? And moreover, why would she want to? "Mr. Klein, this will be a slightly formal affair and—"

"First off," Earl said, leaning forward so far his knees bumped the coffee table, "don't call me Mr. Klein. I've known you practically since you were running down the sidewalk in a diaper, Jenna Pearson, and you've always called me Earl. I don't go for that fancy Mister thing. A man's name should be one word, not two."

The composure that had traveled with her from New York began to slip, not that she'd had such a firm hold on it lately. For years, Jenna had trained herself to be professional, calm, collected. To be a woman firmly in charge of her business and the situation. But in the past few months, that control had slipped out of her grasp, and now, with Betsy glaring at her and Earl throwing out crazy ideas, the last vestiges of control slipped away.

She bit her lip. Refused to cry. Refused to be anything but the can-do party planner she used to be. "Mr...uh, Earl, I really think we should consider something a little more... sit-down for Eunice's birthday party."

"Hell, you sit down to eat your roasted hog, don't you?"

"Yes, but—"

"And Eunice loves pork. Don't she, Betsy?"

Betsy nodded. With enthusiasm. "She does indeed. We all do."

Jenna had come to Riverbend with a nice, neat, typed and comb-bound idea of Eunice Dresden's birthday party. When she'd talked to Betsy on the phone two weeks ago, she'd thought they'd been on the same page. Granted, Betsy had been cantankerous and unsure she wanted Jenna in charge of Eunice's party, but Jenna had been sure once she presented the ideas, Betsy would come around. Somehow, she needed to get this derailed party back on track, without entrées that still had their heads and hooves attached. "I'm not sure a hog roast would work at the Riverbend Function Hall," Jenna said. "It's not quite the location for that kind of thing, and I'm not sure it fits the theme that we decided upon, the one that would celebrate the different decades of Eunice's life. However, we could have something simpler. Italian food, for instance. A nice lasagna—"

"Stockton Grisham!" The name exploded from Betsy's lips, echoed by a slap of her palm against her thigh.

"Stockton Grisham?" His name echoed in Jenna's mind, sent a tingle down her spine—one that she ignored. She'd intended to get through her entire trip without ever mentioning him, and here she'd been in Riverbend less than twenty-four hours and he'd already been the subject of conversation twice.

For a man she'd worked hard to forget, he seemed to be in her every thought. Or at least determined to be there.

"Good idea," Earl said, planting another noisy kiss on Betsy's cheek. She slapped his arm, then blushed. He crooked a grin at her, one that cemented a dimple in his left chin. He scooted his wiry frame a few inches closer to Betsy. "That boy can cook."

"Uh, I don't think—"

"Then it's settled," Betsy said, in that no-argument way she had. "Stockton will make the food. Oh, Eunice is going to be so pleased. She loves Stockton's cooking."

Earl nodded. "Stockton's the only one who can make food Eunice will eat, even when she forgets her teeth at home."

Jenna spent another ten minutes arguing against the use of Stockton as a caterer, but Betsy and Earl were adamant. They were sure no one could cook for the locals like one of their own. "I guess Stockton is our chef," she said finally, biting back a sigh.

A smile spread across Betsy's face, the kind of self-satisfied smile a cat might have once it had a mouse firmly under its paw. "Eunice is my sister, and she means everything to me. You *will* make sure she has the best birthday ever, or you'll never plan another party in this town again."

"It'll be fine," Jenna said. It would, wouldn't it? After all, she'd planned hundreds of parties. She had the experience. It was the confidence that had deserted her in recent months.

She *could* do this. She *would* do this. And in the process, show Betsy and the rest of Riverbend she was more than they'd ever expected her to be.

"Glad to hear it." Betsy patted Jenna's knee. "And I'm so glad Stockton will be a part of this. If anyone knows how to make a woman happy, it's him."

Jenna bit back her disagreement. She needed this job more than she needed to be right.

CHAPTER TWO

"WE'RE CLOSED," STOCKTON called out when he heard the front door of Rustica open. "Come back at eleven, when we start serving lunch."

"I'm not here to eat."

Even from all the way in the back of the restaurant, Stockton recognized the voice. Heard the familiar husky notes. Even now, even after everything, his pulse quickened. Damn.

Stockton took his time laying the ladle in his hands onto the stainless steel counter and removing the apron tied around his waist, before he pushed through the double doors of the kitchen and out into the dining room. And saw her.

Jenna.

His gaze started at the bottom and worked its way up, gliding over the knee-high black leather boots hugging her calves, past the dark green sweater dress clinging to her curves, lingering on the smooth length of her black hair—she'd let it grow out, and now the silky tendrils danced over her shoulders, begging to be touched—and then, finally coming to rest on her heart-shaped face. Big green eyes, the color of jade, and dark red lips that he knew from experience tasted like honey.

She was still beautiful. And undoubtedly still trouble.

The kind of woman who wanted more out of him than he could give.

"Jenna." Her name was almost a whisper, scraping past his throat with the rawness of a word that hadn't been spoken in years. He cleared his throat, tried that again. Why was he still so affected by her? It had to be the passage of time, the shock of seeing her. Nothing more. "How can I help you? Do you need a reservation?"

"I need a chef," she said. "And according to Betsy and Earl, you're the one I should be talking to."

The words were as devoid of emotion as a recipe book. He should have been glad. Their relationship had been over for years, and he wanted to keep it that way. He had his hands full with the restaurant. But for some reason, Jenna's business-like approach ticked him off. "I'm too busy right now to take on anything extra. Thanks for the offer, though." He turned and went back into his kitchen.

The warm, expansive space wrapped around him. The rich scent of fresh spaghetti sauce carried on the air, married by the warm, sweet notes of baking bread. He had chosen every countertop, every plate, every fork, himself. When he walked into Rustica every morning, he knew this place was his. Every inch of it.

The restaurant brought him a solace he hadn't found anywhere else, a peace he wasn't even aware he needed until he held it in his soul.

He'd loved food all his life, and on the rare occasions when his father was home, the two of them had bonded, not over a football in the backyard, but over a plate of lasagna in the kitchen. Stockton had begged his father to let him try his hand with some of the dishes, but Hank Grisham was firm about one thing—the kitchen was his domain, and no one was allowed to handle so much as a ladle but him.

Now Stockton had his own kitchen, and though he didn't ascribe to the same theories as his father, he understood the love Hank had had for his kitchen. Working at Rustica wasn't his job, it was his passion. His days here filled the holes in his nights, gave him something to look forward to, a vocation that completely suited him. He had a job he loved, a business that was doing well, and enough friends and family to fill a boat.

Now Jenna Pearson had walked into his restaurant and disrupted that quiet peace he'd spent years attaining.

The kitchen door swung open with a slight squeak. "You have to take this job, Stockton. I…" She hesitated.

He waited.

"I need you." The three words hung in the air. Her gaze darted away from his and lighted on the stainless steel countertops. "To work for me, I mean."

"Of course. What else could you mean?"

She jerked her attention back to him, a fiery flash in her green eyes. "This is business, pure and simple. I'm planning a party for Eunice Dresden's birthday, and I need a caterer."

He retied the apron around his waist, grabbed a kitchen towel and then crossed to one of the massive ovens to peek inside at the baking bread. Better that than to look at her and say what he really wanted to say—that she had never been about anything other than her career and her future when they'd been together. That her heart had been as remote as the other side of the world, and that distance had kept them from ever becoming truly close. He had no intentions of wrapping himself in that vicious, pointless circle again. "Since I own this place, I choose who I do business with." He withdrew the loaves, then set them on racks to cool. "Today, that's not you."

"Why are you being difficult?"

Because he hadn't been prepared for Jenna Pearson to walk through his front door. Because he knew if he took this job, he'd be spending hours with her. And most of all, because he knew where spending hours with her could lead—to rehashing a past he'd done a darn good job forgetting. He was his father's son in one way—he could whip up a killer coq au vin, but he couldn't make a mixture of business and relationships work.

"It's not a good idea for us to work together." He closed the oven door, then faced her. "Don't you remember how badly things ended between us?"

"That was different. We were young and foolish…and made rash decisions."

Rash decisions. His mind rocketed back to a heady weekend they'd spent in Chicago, a single night of insanity that had been the culmination of a long, hot summer. The last summer before the start of college, the summer he'd thought they were moving forward, when really, they'd been moving apart. An image of Jenna, nestled in the fluffy white comforter that had covered the hotel room bed, her dark hair spread out in an airy cloud around her head, intruded on his mind. He could still smell the vanilla notes of her perfume, a scent that had dusted every surface of the room. Could still feel the hope he'd felt that weekend, before everything had changed.

"I remember," he said, and pushed the memory aside. "I remember everything, Jenna. Do you?"

She ignored the question. "Working together would be different."

He closed the distance between them. "Would it? Really?"

Her chin jutted up. "Of course."

He told himself it would be, that he could provide the food for Eunice's party and not get wrapped up in Jenna again, and was about to say exactly that, when he drew in a breath, and with it, the scent of her perfume. Warm, spicy—

And exactly the same. Every inch of him wanted to trail a kiss along her throat, to taste her skin again. To feel her in his arms, to have Jenna against him. To make a mistake he knew would be monumental.

It had taken him a long time to get over her after they'd broken up. To give up the dream of a future that was never going to happen. To realize that being with her had nearly derailed him from his own plans. And most of all, to realize that if he had stayed with her, he would have ruined her life, as surely as his father had ruined his mother's.

"I don't have time," he said. It was a lie. He could easily make the time if he wanted to.

Operative words—*if* he wanted to.

"Because it's Rustica's first anniversary this month?" She gestured toward the dining room. "I saw the sign."

He'd hung a banner yesterday announcing the restaurant's birthday, and inviting the patrons to a celebration dinner on New Year's Eve. And while, yes, he'd be insanely busy with that, it wasn't the reason he was avoiding her job. Rather than tell Jenna the truth, he leapt on the handy excuse. "That party will consume a lot of my time. I'm sure you can find another caterer in Indianapolis."

Jenna pursed her lips, and crossed her arms over her chest. Avoiding her gaze, he turned out the bread loaves, then put another half dozen balls of dough into bread pans and slid those into the oven. The heat hit him in a thick wave, ebbing when he shut the heavy door again.

"What if I helped?" Jenna said.

Stockton chuckled. "You? Helping me? Cook?"

She shrugged. "I can cook."

"This isn't home ec, Jenna. It's real life." The words came out harsher than he'd intended.

Her gaze darted to the wall of spices, then returned to him. "What about planning your anniversary party? I'm sure you could use a hand with that."

Undoubtedly, Samantha had planted the same seed in Jenna's mind yesterday. "I'm fine. All under control. If I need help, I'll call—"

"This job is important to me, Stockton." She bit her lip, an action he knew meant she was worried. "I really want Eunice's party to go perfectly. It's going to be a huge event, for the whole town."

"Why do you care so much?" He pushed off from the counter and neared her, until he could see the gold flecks in her emerald eyes. Once, her gaze would have affected him. Made him find a way to compromise, to coax a smile from her lips. Those days were over. "Last I knew, you wanted to stay as far from this town as possible."

And me, but he didn't add that.

"Because..." She took in a breath, let it out, and he got the feeling whatever she was about to say was coming from some place deep inside her that she rarely visited, that side of herself that held the honest assessment of her life. He'd known Jenna Pearson since first grade, and knew she wasn't a woman who liked self-analysis. "Because I want to prove to this town that I made it, that my business is capable and successful."

Something in her words didn't ring true, but he couldn't figure out what. "And you had to leave New York to do that?"

A frown knitted her brows. "I'm here, and I need a caterer. That's really all you need to know."

"I hope you find someone," he said, returning to his sauces. "Whatever caterer you use, Eunice will undoubtedly be happy with the food. Because last I checked, it was the thought that counted when it came to parties, not the lasagna."

Jenna sat at one of the small rectangular tables in the dining room of Rustica, a hot cup of coffee she'd poured herself sitting on the white linen tablecloth. Delicate tendrils of steam filled the air. The steam only added to the tension still hanging in the air, a storm she'd stirred up from the minute she saw Stockton Grisham again.

Drat that man. Even after all these years apart, he could still push the wrong buttons.

She should have left. Should have gone down to Indianapolis and found another caterer, as Stockton had told her to. Hell, she shouldn't have come here in the first place, knowing she'd see him again.

She had to admit, Stockton had done an amazing job with the restaurant. It embodied his personality, yet maintained an authentic Italian feel. Rustica's décor was filled with rich russet hues, offset by the antique water jugs lining a shelf near the ceiling, and the multicolored hand-made round platters mounted above the booths. Stockton had created a warm, inviting atmosphere. Not too dark, not too light and definitely not too kitschy. No wonder he'd been such a success.

If she'd been another person, she would have been envious that he had made it—and she had lost what success she'd had. But she wasn't. She'd known Stockton forever, and his success was well-deserved. It was what he had wanted—what he had always wanted.

More than he'd wanted her.

She shrugged off the thoughts. She didn't have time to dwell on the past. She toyed with the hot mug, and considered her options. It didn't take long. She had none.

Her business in New York was nearly defunct. The last few jobs had been disasters, with one thing after another going wrong. Caterers who didn't show up, florists who delivered the wrong stems, bands whose music disappointed. The word hadn't taken long to spread, and before she knew it, her growing party planning business was almost dead.

Somewhere along the way, she'd lost her mojo. Every day, she woke up, faced the mirror and told herself that the pity party was over. That she would get this business, and by extension, her life, back on track.

But for some reason Jenna couldn't pinpoint, she kept derailing. Her passion for party planning had deflated, and every time she tried to go back to the way things had been before—before the day that turned her life upside down—she got even more lost.

She glanced at the closed kitchen door and decided no more. She would turn things around with this party. No matter what. Jenna got to her feet, crossed to the unattended bar and poured herself another cup of coffee.

"I thought you were leaving."

Stockton's voice drew her up. She took her time returning to the table. "You're the one Eunice wants. I'm not leaving until we've arrived at equitable terms."

Stockton laughed, the sound sharp and bitter. "Equitable terms? Is that we're doing now? Working out a contract?"

"I like to work with a contract. It's standard business practice."

He placed his hands on the table and leaned so close, she couldn't help but inhale the woodsy notes of his cologne. Not the same scent as before, and she had to wonder who had picked out the new cologne. A wife? No, his left hand was bare. A girlfriend? Or Stockton himself?

"Nothing between us has ever been standard. Or

business-like," Stockton said. Jenna started to speak and he stopped her by laying a piece of paper on the table. "I assume you aren't as familiar with this area as you used to be—" he paused a beat, long enough to make sure she got the hidden meaning, that she had been away too long to know much about anything or anyone here in Riverbend "—and so I took the liberty of writing down the names of a few chefs I would recommend. I suggest you call one of them." He picked up her still full coffee cup and left the room. The double doors of the kitchen swung into place with a deep thud-thud.

Jenna glanced at the list. She considered picking it up, and taking the easy way out by calling someone else. Her hand hovered over the white sheet, but in the end, she left it where it was. Eunice and Betsy wanted Stockton. If pleasing the client meant getting Stockton to agree, then that was what she'd have to do. Clearly, it was going to take more work than she'd expected.

Jenna grabbed her purse and walked out of Rustica. It wouldn't do any good to stay and keep arguing with him. She needed time to think, to figure out a way to bring Stockton around to her point of view.

Had she really thought it would be that easy? That she could just walk in there and convince Stockton to do what she wanted, as if they had never dated? Never had that turbulent breakup?

Jenna drove the few miles from Rustica to her aunt's house and worked on a plan. There had to be something she could leverage with Stockton. As she pulled into the driveway, she flipped out her cell, first dialing the number for her business voice mail. Maybe there'd be good news. A bunch of potential clients interested in booking parties through her, or a satisfied customer leaving a recommendation. But no...there were only two messages, one from a creditor and one from a client—canceling her upcoming anniversary event, the only other booking on Jenna's calendar for the next three months. Through the woman's sobs, Jenna gathered the marriage was over, and thus, the need for a tenth-anniversary party was, too.

Deep breath. This wasn't the end of the world. She had a booked event right here in Riverbend. One that would be a success, on every level.

With that newly cemented resolve in place, Jenna placed another call. A moment later, a cheery hello greeted her. "Livia. I'm so glad you're home." Of course, where else would Livia be? She used to work for Jenna, until business dried up, and she'd been forced to let her assistant go last week.

Olivia Perkins laughed, a light airy sound that seemed a million miles away from the worries crowding Jenna's shoulders. "Hey, Jenna! I've been wondering how you were faring in the backwoods of Indiana."

"Riverbend's not exactly the backwoods. We have a stoplight."

"A stoplight? As in one?" She could hear Livia shaking her head on the other end. "Tell me you at least have running water and electricity."

"Oh, no. It's all water pumps and gas lanterns here."

Livia laughed again. "Remind me never to vacation there."

"Actually…" Jenna let out a breath. "I was hoping you'd fly in and help me out."

"I thought you said this was a job you could handle with one hand tied behind your back."

She'd said that—before she'd encountered Betsy's resistance. Before she'd realized she'd be working with Stockton Grisham. And before her entire plan for the party had blown up before she got so much as one napkin in place.

A part of her worried that this simple birthday party would fall apart, just like the Martin wedding and the Turner Insurance Christmas party. And her plans for her great comeback would derail, as surely as her business had in the past few months. Her confidence, which used to be as solid as granite, had been shaken over the past few months, and she couldn't seem to get it back.

Damn it, she would. She refused to let this…this *funk*… last another minute.

"You're right," she told Livia. "This job's a piece of cake. I just had a crazy moment of doubt."

"Aw, Jenna, that's normal. You'll be fine, I'm sure."

"Thanks for the vote of confidence." Jenna ran a hand through her hair. Outside her car, a light snow began to fall. Snowflakes danced across the glass then slid onto the wipers. "Once I convince the caterer that working with us is in his best interests, it'll be downhill from there."

"Show him some of that Jenna Pearson determination. The same moxie you used to build your business. That man will be putty in your hands."

Jenna let out a laugh. "You haven't met Stockton Grisham. He's not so easily swayed." A tightness grew in her gut at the mention of his name. Why did she care? The last thing she'd come to Riverbend for was to reopen old wounds and past relationships. Work—that was her only focus.

On the other end of the phone, Jenna heard the click of keys on a keyboard, and Livia hmm-hmming for a moment. "It's probably not much help, but how about I come down on New Year's Eve?"

"Don't you have some hot date in the city?"

Livia sighed. "No. I broke up with Paul last week. I'm officially single again."

"Sorry, Liv."

"I'm not. Who needs a guy who looks in the mirror more than he does at his date?" Livia laughed. "Hey, you never know. I might just find Mr. Right in your one-stoplight town."

"If you do, let me know." Maybe Livia would have better odds than Jenna, who'd only found Mr. Definitely-not-Right here.

"No problem," Livia said. "I'll see you at the airport on New Year's Eve. Until then, chin up. You'll do fine."

The support rallied Jenna's flagging spirits. She could tackle this—and definitely tackle the Stockton Grisham... problem. "Thanks, Livia. You're the best."

"No," Livia said softly. "Just a good friend who knows when another friend is in trouble. Even if she doesn't want to admit it."

CHAPTER THREE

STOCKTON THOUGHT HE had seen the last of Jenna. Hell, he'd thought that eight years ago, and clearly he'd been wrong. Because she was back in his restaurant again. After yesterday, he was sure she'd abandon this insane plan of having him work with her.

Not that he wouldn't love to give Eunice, one of his favorite customers, a birthday to remember. And in the process, secure a little more business for Rustica, and spread the restaurant's name with the guests at the party, many of whom were undoubtedly coming in from out of town. Even though the restaurant had had a successful first year, it never hurt to keep growing the business. A party like Eunice's, filled with people who hadn't yet tried Rustica, could do that.

It wasn't the job itself, or the money he'd make, it was the price he'd have to pay—working side by side with Jenna for several days. Remembering how things used to be, how he'd once hoped for a future with her, and how badly things had soured. Surely she could find a caterer in Indiana she didn't share a history with. He'd go back to concentrating on his restaurant, and she'd eventually go back to New York—and he'd forget all about her again.

The plan sounded good in theory. But as his front door opened and Jenna walked into his restaurant for the second time in two days, he realized a plan was no good unless it was executed by both parties. Clearly, Jenna was reading from a different plan book than him.

She strode up to him, fire in her eyes, a set to her jaw that he knew as well as he knew his own name. He'd seen that same look back in high school when she'd had control of the ball on the soccer field, and blown past four opponents like she was brushing mosquitoes off her shoulder. The same look she used to get on her face when she'd been on the debate team and up against a particularly daunting opponent. The same look that had come over her face when she'd applied for a job at a banquet hall in a nearby town and the owner had told her she didn't have what it took to work in event planning. Stockton knew that look meant one thing—

She wasn't leaving here until she had what she wanted.

"I know what you said yesterday, but I'd like you to reconsider." She held up a hand to cut off his protests. "If you provide the food for this party, it would be great for your business."

"You said that yesterday. And I told you then that my business is doing just fine, thank you."

"Every business could stand to grow and expand its customer base."

He leaned back against the smooth oak surface of Rustica's bar and crossed his arms over his chest. He forced his gaze to her face, away from the enticing curves beneath her black V-neck blouse and dark skirt. Everything she was wearing was more suitable for a boardroom than a few days in Riverbend, where casual attire ruled the day, but he'd be lying if he said he wasn't intrigued by the understated sexiness in her clothing choices. She had on high-heeled black pumps that seemed to beg a man to keep his attention on her legs. Beg every man but him. "Even your business?"

"Well, of course." A flush filled her cheeks, then she shook her head and seemed to will the crimson from her face.

Stockton leaned forward, waiting until her gaze met his. In those deep green depths, he saw something he had missed the day before.

A lie.

"Why are you really doing this party?"

"Because Betsy wants her sister to have a happy birthday."

"You've never much cared for Betsy. Or she for you, if I remember my Halloweens correctly. And from the scuttle-butt I hear around town, she's not too keen on the idea of you running this shindig."

Jenna looked away. "The people in this town have always liked to talk."

Regret rocketed through him. His mouth had gotten away from his brain, and he needed to reel it back in. Jenna Pearson, of all people, wouldn't want to hear what the busybodies of this town had to say. Still, for her to battle such odds, there had to be something more than a party behind her return to Riverbend. "Tell me the real reason you're here."

That lower jaw set again, and a muscle ticked in her cheeks. She was fuming, but she wasn't going to show it to him. "Because I haven't seen my aunt in forever, and this seemed like a great opportunity to come back and visit with her."

"Half the truth," Stockton said, "is not the same as the full truth."

"I do have a job catering Eunice's birthday party. I did

think it would be nice to see my aunt again. It's a win-win. Nothing more."

He could see the lie in her eyes. Hear it in the strain in her voice. But why? And about what? He thought of pressing her on it, then decided to drop the subject. "Did you call any of the other caterers on the list I gave you?" He already knew that answer—after she left, he'd noticed the paper still sitting on the table.

She shook her head. "I don't want any of them. I want you."

The words slammed into him with a fierce electric rush. In Chicago all those years ago, he'd heard her whisper those same words in his ear, then she'd kissed a trail down his throat, over his chest, until he hauled her up into his arms and off to bed.

But the reasons why she'd said them then, and why she was now, were very, very different.

"I'm not available," he said.

Were they talking about business? Or something more?

"Stockton!"

He pivoted. Grace, the hostess, was standing in the kitchen, waving at him from across the room. "What's up?"

"Larry called in sick *again*." She made a little face, then ducked back into the kitchen to avoid the coming storm.

Stockton cursed. Three times in one week. "That man better have a fatal disease," he called to Grace, even though she was already gone. He turned back to Jenna. "I have to go."

"Wait!" Before he could walk away, Jenna lay a hand on his arm. The touch seared his skin, sent his hormones tumbling through his veins and rocketed his mind back again to the first and only time they'd made love.

Images of Jenna's naked body beneath his, her skin warm against his chest, his legs, flashed in his mind. He pushed the thoughts away. Thinking of the past would do him no good. Not now.

Not ever.

He glanced down at her delicate hand, firm on his arm. As if she realized what she'd done, Jenna jerked away. "I have to get into the kitchen," he said.

"What if…what if I helped?"

"Helped what?"

"Fill Larry's shoes. Just for tonight."

He smirked. "You. Do Larry's job."

"Sure. I mean, I waited tables in college for a couple months. It can't be that much different from—"

"Larry is my sous chef."

"Oh." Her eyes widened, and she took a half-step back. "Oh, well…"

"Exactly. Now, if you'll excuse me—"

Her hand latched on to his arm again. Why did something so simple still affect him? Half of him wanted to turn around and crush her to his chest, the other half wanted to fling off her hand and tell her not to open a Pandora's Box she didn't intend to shut again.

He did neither.

"I may not be the best sous chef in the world, but I'm sure I can be more of a help in the kitchen than not having a right hand man at all. And, I'll throw in free party-planning advice for your anniversary event. Surely, you can't turn down an offer like that." She shot him a tempting grin.

"And what, I'd owe you after that?" He shook his head, and tugged his arm out of her hand. "I don't think so. I know you, Jenna. You make it sound like you're here to help me out, but really, you're just running your own agenda."

She winced, and he wanted to take the words back, but

they were out there. The harsh truth, in broad daylight. "It's just one dinner service, Stockton. Nothing more."

He was about to say no, and in fact had the syllable formed on his tongue, when he thought of the night ahead. One that would surely be insanely fast-paced, as had the night before.

At least it was Thursday. It would undoubtedly be busy—the longer the week wore on, the busier the restaurant got, and with it being the holidays, people were in more often during the week. If Larry missed Friday, or Saturday, or worse, Sunday—New Year's Eve—well, Stockton wasn't going to think about that. Midweek was bad enough to be down an essential pair of hands.

Last night, Stockton had run the kitchen single-handedly, overworking the two prep chefs and himself trying to keep the orders moving in a timely manner, but they'd done it and managed not to screw up any orders. Stockton had gone home exhausted and cranky, as had the rest of the overworked staff. A second night of the same didn't sound appealing at all. Not to mention the reaction of the prep chefs when they found out they'd be doing double duty again. With the anniversary party so near, he couldn't afford to lose any of his help. Nor did he have time to interview and hire someone else.

"You can't cook," he said to Jenna.

"I'm not as bad as you remember," she said, and a part of him wondered again if they were talking about cooking or something else. "Let me help you, Stockton."

He could almost believe she was sincere, if he tried hard enough. But he knew Jenna Pearson—and knew she wasn't making the offer out of the goodness of her heart. She wanted to butter him up to convince him to say yes to catering Eunice's party. Or maybe something more.

The kitchen door banged open, and Denny, one of the

prep chefs, came storming into the front of the house. "Don't tell me we're shorthanded again tonight. I swear, I'm going to go to Larry's house and drag him—"

"We won't be shorthanded," Stockton said. The decision formed in his head. Whether he liked it or not, he had to take the deal on the table. He couldn't afford another night like last night.

"Larry showed up?"

"No," Stockton said, then turned to Jenna and gave her a short nod. "I hired some help. *Temporary* help."

Denny looked between Stockton and Jenna, taking in the ruffled blouse, the snug fit skirt, her high heels, none of which were appropriate for the hot, busy kitchen. He arched a brow in disbelief, then shrugged. "Whatever you say, boss." He hurried back into the kitchen, undoubtedly to tell the rest of the staff that the head chef had gone crazy.

"So we have a deal?" Jenna asked.

"First, you go home and change into something appropriate for the kitchen. Sneakers, a T-shirt. Put your hair back. Then come back here, ready to work."

"I didn't bring anything like that with me."

"You won't last five minutes in my kitchen in that," he said, waving at her skirt and heels. "And you should know by now that you won't last long in Riverbend looking like you walked off the pages of a fashion magazine."

She opened her mouth to argue. Shut it again. "I'll buy something else to wear."

"Good. Be here at four."

"Do you promise you'll let me talk to you about catering for Eunice's birthday party?"

"We'll see how you work out," he said, already wondering if he'd made the right decision. Jenna, in his kitchen, underfoot, all night? What had he been thinking? "I like my help to have staying power. And not run at the first sign of confrontation."

Her gaze narrowed, and he knew she realized he wasn't talking about cooking. "Unlike other people I know," she said, "you can depend on me, Stockton." She gathered up her coat and purse, and twisted her scarf around her neck. "More than you think."

Betsy was waiting in Aunt Mabel's kitchen. She looked like a Christmas tree gone awry, with her bright green sweater topped by embroidered silver snowflakes, and a matching pair of fleece pants. The only thing lacking from her festive attire was a smile. Dread filled Jenna's chest.

She took a deep breath. These were the people who had known her all her life, not ordinary clients. Whatever they had to say she could handle. For goodness' sake, it was a birthday party, not a wedding for five hundred.

"There's been a...development." Betsy took a sip from her mug and eyed Jenna over the porcelain rim. Outside, snow began to fall. Fluffy white flakes danced on the slight breeze, kissed the windows, then dropped away.

"A development?" Jenna forced a smile to her face, and took the seat opposite Betsy.

Aunt Mabel poured Jenna a cup of coffee and joined the other two. "Now, Betsy, don't exaggerate," she said. "This is hardly a problem."

Betsy pursed her lips. "I disagree. We need to rethink the entire event."

"Whatever the issue is, Miss Williams, I'm sure we can make the necessary changes and ensure the party goes off without a—"

"What happened with the Marshall wedding?"

Oh, God. Not that one, of all events. Jenna had thought coming back to Indiana meant she could leave her business past behind, that she could get a much-needed fresh start, one she could parlay into a comeback. How had Betsy found out about the Marshall wedding?

It didn't matter—she knew, as did most of New York. The debutante's wedding that had turned into a disaster of epic proportions, and ended up starring on all the gossip pages for several days afterward. Jenna should have known better than to think she could handle such a huge event after all the others that had gone wrong. If she'd been smart, she would have handed the reins over to Livia. Stepped aside.

"That event, uh, didn't go as well as I expected," Jenna said.

"I heard that the flowers didn't arrive, and the bride's brother ended up running out to the local supermarket to get some for the corsages and things. Now, here in Indiana, maybe something as simple as store flowers might be fine. But from what I read, that wasn't what the bride pictured for her wedding at that fancy-dancy hotel."

"There was an issue with the booking date for the florist. But I solved the problem." By scrambling to find another florist she'd worked with several times before, calling in a huge favor and paying a premium to have arrangements rushed over at the last possible second.

"Did the limo driver also get the date wrong? And the caterer?" Betsy asked. "The bride was quite upset about serving pizza to her guests. At least the pizza parlor threw in free soda so people had something to drink."

Jenna remembered the bride's screaming fit—a justified reaction—and all directed at the party planner who had ruined the wedding by scheduling all the vendors for the following weekend. Jenna remembered thinking she had it all under control, that she was doing great. And then the day of the wedding arrived and proved she was as wrong as she could be.

She'd thought the next job, and the one after that, and the one after that, would bring her back to her normal, organized, Type-A self. They hadn't. If anything, the mistakes had gotten bigger, the stress blossoming larger in her chest.

And now, all those mistakes had followed her to Riverbend. The one place she'd thought she could escape from everything.

Jenna sighed, and sat back in her seat. Aunt Mabel reached out, and placed a consoling hand on her niece's shoulder. "I made a few mistakes with that one," she said, "but everything was rectified in the end."

"Is that something you do often? Make mistakes?" Betsy leaned in, and Jenna got the feeling she was a bug under a microscope, about to get squashed by the scientist's lens. "Because I looked your business up on Google this morning," Betsy went on, "and I have to say I was shocked, Jenna Pearson. Quite shocked. Your aunt told me you were a great party planner. The best, in fact."

She had been a great party planner once. And she could be again, she told herself. One success—that was all she needed. "I've had some problems in the past few months, some…issues I've been dealing with. But things are on the upswing."

"Betsy, everyone has off days," Aunt Mabel said. "You need to be more understanding."

"We all have rough days, weeks, even months, Mabel," Betsy said. "I myself have had some days that were less than sunny, but I never served my guests pizza instead of a good home-cooked meal." She pursed her lips and looked ready to cancel the party at any second.

Silence blanketed the table. Betsy was right. Jenna had

let down her clients, the people who had trusted her. These were monumental events in their lives, and she had turned them into disasters.

Maybe she had lost her touch. Maybe she shouldn't be doing this job anymore. "You're right, Miss Williams. In the past, I made several mistakes. But I'm back on my feet now, and prepared to do the best job I can with Eunice's party." She could do this, she knew she could. Especially here, in Riverbend where the expectations were less demanding, the people happy with a "plain and simple" affair, as Betsy had said. She could handle plain and simple.

And then, after the party, be ready to return to New York, to the life she used to love, the job she used to be great at, and get back on top in no time.

"I'm not so sure about that," Betsy said. "In fact, perhaps I better make backup plans just in case."

"You don't need—"

"I think I do. People say the apples don't fall from the trees. I know the tree your family comes from, Jenna Pearson, and I think—"

"Betsy!" Aunt Mabel interrupted. "That's enough."

"Fine. But you have to know I love my sister," Betsy said. "More than all the tea in China. And if she ends up eating pizza instead of Stockton's lasagna, I'll put you on toilet-cleaning duty at the bed and breakfast for the next fifty years."

CHAPTER FOUR

THE FIRST HOUR WAS the hardest. Even though both the prep cooks were already there and busy in the kitchen, Stockton's radar attuned to one station. Jenna Pearson.

Every move she made, he noted. Every time she brushed past him to reach for a spice or a utensil, he caught a whiff of her perfume. The same scent she'd worn years ago, a warm, heady perfume with notes of vanilla, cinnamon. His gaze traveled her frame more than once, and he found himself wondering if she'd feel the same in his arms, if she'd taste the same under his lips.

Then he'd stop, get a grip and get back to work. There'd be no getting wrapped up with her, not again.

In the end, she wanted things he didn't. When they'd been younger, he'd been consumed by wanderlust. He'd thought only of leaving the small, confining boundaries of Riverbend and traveling the world, thinking— Well, hell, thinking he'd find more. Find the relationship with his father that he'd always craved. Find the secret to success. After two years of traveling, he'd realized one thing. That being home was the key to all of that. For him, Riverbend was home. For Jenna, it was anything but.

It wasn't about the town. He could understand why Jenna might not want to settle here, of all places. It was that they were two weathervanes, pointing in opposite directions.

What he craved now—community, purpose, home—had never interested her. At least he'd found that out years ago, before he could make a foolish mistake that would have hurt them both in the end.

He turned back to making soup, a far safer proposition—and with far more predictable results.

He rolled up several basil leaves and danced the knife down the green bundle, creating a quick chiffonade. Then he turned and dumped the freshly cut herb into a minestrone simmering on the stove. Across the kitchen, Jenna was peeling potatoes and dropping them into a pot of cold water. The prep chefs pretended not to eavesdrop, but Stockton was no fool. The kitchen was small, and nearly every conversation became a public event.

"So, what's your plan for the anniversary party?" Jenna asked.

"I've ordered some balloons. Put the customer favorites on the menu and I hired a DJ." He stirred and tasted the soup. He sprinkled in a little more salt, gave the pepper mill a few turns, then tasted again. Perfect. He moved on to starting the vinaigrette that dressed all the house salads at Rustica.

"That's it?"

"Sounds like enough to me. It's a party, not a White House dinner."

Jenna arched a brow, the kind that said the man didn't have a clue. "If you don't mind my saying so, I think you could take it up a notch...or ten."

He whisked oil into vinegar, his movements fast, creating a smooth emulsion of flavors. As he did, he couldn't help but think about the oil and vinegar of him and Jenna. "Do you like New York?" he asked.

The change of subject took her by surprise. She stopped

peeling for a moment and looked at him. "I like it well enough. Why?"

Because I want to know if it was worth it. Because I want to know if you found there what you could never seem to find here.

Even as the thoughts danced in his mind, a part of him questioned whether he had done the same. Had he found what he'd been looking for? What he'd wandered the world to find, and come back here, thinking everything he ever wanted was here.

"Just wondering." He sprinkled in some minced fresh herbs, and whisked some more. "Must be pretty different from Riverbend."

She laughed. "Most definitely." Then she paused, the peeler poised over a fat white potato. "But in some ways, it's very much like Riverbend."

"How's that?"

"New York isn't so much a city as a collection of little neighborhoods. It's like having dozens of small towns, all butted up against each other. When you move into an apartment in SoHo or Greenwich Village or the Lower East Side, that little pocket of the city has its own flavor."

"And its own quirky residents."

A smile danced across her features. "Oh, there are plenty of those."

"Just like here."

"Yeah." The word exhaled on a breath.

He knew what she was leaving unsaid. He let the subject alone. Jenna's years in Riverbend had been tough. First with the loss of her parents, then with the whispers that had followed her around for years, a persistent shadow to her personal tragedy.

"I'm surprised you had time to come down here and do

Eunice's party," he said, shifting the subject again. "Your company must be really busy in a city like New York."

Jenna flipped the half-peeled potato over and over in her palm. "My business has been struggling for a while."

He blinked, then took a moment to absorb what she'd said. "Your business is struggling? But I thought—"

"Well, you thought wrong. Things always look different from half a country away." She bent her head and went back to peeling potatoes. Long strips of dark skins flipped away from the furious movements of her hands.

In other words, he'd been too far away from her to have a clear picture of what was going on in her life. To be expected, considering how little contact they'd had after the breakup. A Christmas card or two, a mailed-back forgotten CD, a couple of phone calls. They'd dropped off the face of each other's worlds. And though it had been painful, because he couldn't remember a day when he hadn't had Jenna in his life, it had been the best decision all around.

Except now Stockton wondered what he had been missing. When he'd gotten on the plane to Italy, he'd had one last conversation with Jenna. She'd been breezy on the phone, her plate piled high with looking for new business, catering to the clients she'd just signed. She'd landed a couple of corporate accounts right off the bat, then her first wedding, pushing her up the hill of success quickly. He'd tried to call her twice more after that, but got only her answering machine. She'd been gone, lost to the consuming power of entrepreneurship. Gone to him, if she ever was his to begin with.

Now, after owning his own business, he could understand that single-minded focus, but at the time, he'd been seriously hurt. If anything had cemented their breakup, it had been that. Jenna off in New York, moved on to a new life.

One that no longer included him.

He'd gone to Italy, staying for a while with his father and Hank's second wife, then wandered the countryside, working for pay and sometimes for free for other chefs, honing his culinary skills. It had been an adventure unlike any other, one filled with tastes and smells and good Italian hospitality. By the time he'd returned to Riverbend, he'd found his center again, and decided leaving Jenna to her life was the best decision all around.

Except…occasionally those nagging doubts returned to whisper in his ear. He'd found the perfect place for his restaurant, yes. Found success. But there was something… something intangible…lacking still. The old itch to wander returned, but Stockton shrugged it off. Running would do him no good. Especially with his business about to celebrate its anniversary.

"Italy was like that, too," he said, changing gears once again, trying to avoid the tense bumps in the conversational road. "The towns are small and cozy, and every neighborhood had its own special touch. Even its own food. The lasagna I tasted in one part of Italy was just a tiny bit different in another place."

Jenna picked up her last potato and started peeling it. "Did you spend a lot of time with your father there?"

"No."

"I thought when you left—"

"You thought wrong." He scowled. He didn't like unrest in his kitchen, and now here he was, causing plenty of it. Regret flooded him. "I'm sorry. It's just my father has never been what I'd call supportive."

"I heard he owns a restaurant in Italy now."

Stockton nodded. "He thinks the only place you can have a truly successful restaurant is in either a big city or a country dedicated to culinary excellence. Indiana doesn't fit the bill in either of those categories."

"He's never been to Rustica?"

Stockton shook his head. "I suppose he doesn't want me to prove him wrong."

"If you ask me, he's the one who's missing out. It's a great restaurant, Stockton. The food is amazing. I want to eat everything that leaves this kitchen." She paused, and her gaze met his. "You've really done it."

"Thank you."

She fiddled with the potato peeler. Behind him, Stockton heard the bustle of the kitchen as the staff readied the restaurant for the night's onslaught. "Why did you choose Riverbend, though? You could have opened a restaurant anywhere. Even...New York."

Where she had been. He could hear the underlying question—why hadn't he followed her to the big city and embarked on his dream there? He, the one who had all that urge to travel, and had ultimately ended up back at where they'd both started? "Because I didn't have any ties to New York."

The truth sat there between them, cold and stark. He wanted to take it back, make up something else, but he didn't.

"Of course," Jenna said, and went back to the potatoes.

"It was more than that," Stockton went on, and wondered why it was suddenly so important to him that Jenna understood. "I love this town. I used to think my father was right, that the only place to have a truly successful restaurant was in the heart of a city or a renowned culinary country. But the more I traveled, the more I realized one thing."

She paused in her work. "What's that?"

"That what makes a restaurant successful isn't just the food or the location. It's the people who patronize it. A good chef learns to listen to his customers, and in turn, they shape the menu, the décor, but more, the mood. I always wanted a restaurant where everyone could feel at home."

"A neighborhood destination?"

He nodded. "Exactly." He thought of his father again and how Hank would never understand Stockton's approach to business. Hank was a man who couldn't even invite his own family into his kitchen. He'd never see the joy of letting the customers shape the restaurant.

"But there are a lot bigger markets out there than Riverbend, Indiana," Jenna said.

"There are. I've visited many of them, worked in a few. The more I did that, though, the more I realized this is exactly the size success I wanted, Jenna. Not everyone wants to be the biggest." He waved to indicate the restaurant beyond the double doors of the kitchen, with its intimate tables, soft lighting, amber tones. "This is exactly what I always dreamed of having. Not too big, and just busy enough to pay the bills but still let me have a life. Someday, I'll be able to settle down, have a family."

Then why had he avoided that so far? Why had he shied away from serious relationships?

Jenna fiddled with the peeler, spinning it round and round in her fingers. "So, you have everything you want now?"

"Pretty much." He dismissed the questions in his mind, then met her gaze. "The question is whether you do."

"Whether I what?"

"Have everything you want." A breath passed between them. "Do you, Jenna?"

She glanced away, quickly. "Uh, the last potato is done. I better get these on the stove for you." She dropped the peeler to the counter and went to lift the heavy pot onto the counter. Stockton crossed to her, his hands going to the handles. They touched, and he lifted his gaze to hers. Damn, she was still beautiful. Still had that way of looking at him that seemed to peer into his soul. Their fingers held the contact a moment longer, then Jenna broke away. "Thanks."

"It's nothing." Who was he trying to convince? Himself? Or her?

"Please cater Eunice's party," Jenna said. "I need you to do this for me, Stockton, regardless of everything between us."

Here they were, back to business again. In the comfort zone both of them liked to maintain.

He wanted to say no. He'd already spent an hour in the kitchen with her, and the whole time, a simmering tension had hung in the air. All those tangled threads that came with sharing a past with someone. If they spent enough time together, eventually one of them would be tempted to pick up a thread.

But as he looked at her, standing a few feet away, he noticed a tension in her shoulders, a worried line across her brow. He suspected she'd understated the trouble her business was in, especially if she'd taken a job here, of all places.

She needed him, she'd said. He'd never thought he'd hear those words from her again. And this week, he'd heard it twice.

The first time she'd said she needed him, he thought it had been a ploy. But now, reading Jenna's body language and the unspoken words in her tone, he realized she was telling the truth. It was more than to help out her struggling business, he suspected, but what more he couldn't discern.

The spurned lover in him could easily say no, just because. But he thought of how hard she had worked to convince him to say yes, and how much it must have taken to come to him, of all people, for help. Once, they had been friends, and that long-held urge to help her returned. Even as his better sense screamed out a warning, Stockton put down the pot and crossed to Jenna. Her green eyes met his, filled with hope, the kind he couldn't resist, no matter how hard he tried. "Seems you've just hired a caterer."

CHAPTER FIVE

THE DINNER RUSH WAS in full swing. Stockton allowed the work to become his sole focus. He bustled around the kitchen, calling out orders, sautéing steaks, grilling vegetables, boiling fresh pasta.

Avoiding Jenna.

For her part, she steered clear of him, too. They shared few words—only enough for him to give her direction and send her off to complete some small kitchen task. At some point, they would have to finish talking, not just about the plan for his anniversary party, but also the menu for Eunice's birthday, and work on bringing those plans together. Until then, there was work.

Work had been his salvation, his distraction, his life, for so long that Stockton had forgotten what normalcy was like. He ate, slept and breathed the restaurant. Spent more hours here than he probably had to, and spent his free time whipping up new recipes. In the early months of the restaurant, he'd had no social life. To be honest, he still had no social life.

Everything had been about building the business, growing the clientele and creating a stand-out environment. There would be time later to have the life he had put on hold. For a long time, he hadn't minded that delay. But lately—

He'd been wondering if maybe he was missing something. If maybe he should take more time off, consider making enough time to have a relationship with more than a knife and a cutting board.

For that reason alone, he'd decided having Jenna's help on planning the anniversary party was a smart idea. It would free up some of Stockton's time, and take a little of the pressure off his shoulders. After thinking about it, he'd realized his minimal plans could use a little wow factor, something Jenna specialized in creating. Surely, he could work on a couple of events with her and keep everything professional.

The acrid scent of something burning filled the air, and Stockton whirled toward the stove. He turned off the burner, removed the scorched pan, filled it with hot water and soap, and set it in the sink to soak, all in the fast, practiced moves of someone who had encountered that emergency a time or ten. "What happened?"

"Uh, a béchamel sauce gone awry?" Jenna offered him up an apologetic smile. "I said I could cook, not create a masterpiece. I guess I thought I had white sauces under control."

"Well, at least we know you can *burn*," he said, chuckling. "Maybe I should have you searing the steaks."

She laughed, then ran the back of her hand over her forehead. "This is a lot harder than I expected."

"You get used to it. Work here long enough and you develop a rhythm." Stockton retrieved another pot from the shelf and set it on the stove.

She gave the pan a dubious glance. "Does that mean you don't burn things anymore?"

He laughed. "I wish. Normally, when I do, it's because I'm trying to do too many things at one time."

"You always did," she said softly, and for a moment, he

could almost believe they were back to old times. To those high school days when his heart leapt at the sight of her, and his every thought centered around touching her.

For the first time, Stockton wondered if this older Jenna—a woman as dedicated to her own career and dreams as he was—would understand this older, more settled version of him.

Or maybe he and Jenna were too similar. Maybe there was something to that adage about opposites attracting. If that was so, then someone better tell his hormones because they weren't paying attention to anything other than her.

"Multitasking is a necessity in this field. You need to be able to talk, listen and manage two or three dishes, all at the same time." He gestured toward the pan. "Let's try the sauce again." Back to work. Always back to work.

"You are a harsh taskmaster." She gathered the butter and flour, then stepped back. When Stockton didn't move in to start the sauce, she gave him an uncertain glance. "You sure you want me to do this again? After I burned the last one? Isn't it better for me to watch you?"

"You can do this." He pushed the butter closer to her. "And when we get busy with customers in a little while, I won't have time to show you. You have to do it for yourself to truly learn."

And for him to be able to walk away, and bury himself in the kitchen instead of in whatever she was doing. Already, being this close to her had him distracted, and that was a bad sign.

She wrinkled her nose, but didn't protest further. Instead, she crossed to the pan, slid the stick of butter into it, then stepped back to wait for it to melt before adding the flour and seasoning.

"Now, whisk," he said.

She did as he said, picking up the stainless steel whisk,

and stirring the roux before Stockton moved in beside her and began adding milk. As soon as he did, he realized he should have had her make that liquid addition. Not just because she needed the experience, but because the sheer act of pouring the liquid put him within inches of her. All evening, he'd done a good job of maintaining distance between them—a few feet, a countertop, a stand mixer. Something that he could use as a wall to tamp down his awareness of her every move, every breath.

A lone tendril of her black hair had escaped the clip she'd used, and it curled along her neck, sweet and tantalizing. He wanted to capture that lock in his fingers, feel it slide silkily through his grasp. His gaze drifted over her neck, swooping down the hollows of her throat. Desire curled tight in his gut.

He swallowed hard and pushed the feeling away. Wanting Jenna had never been a problem. Making a relationship work between them had.

Right now, the last thing he had time for was a complicated involvement, particularly one he knew wasn't going to end happily. He'd learned his lesson long ago. A smart man didn't require multiple trips down Bad Experience Avenue to learn to make a detour.

"Uh, here," he said, nearly shoving the container of milk into her hands. "You should do this."

She glanced over at him, and a smile curved up her face. Damn. Why did she have to smile? "Don't tell me you're abandoning me. You saw what happened last time I tried this on my own."

"I'll be right here."

"Watching me screw up?"

"Something like that."

He'd wanted Jenna Pearson from the minute his hormones matured and he realized the girl he'd known since first grade wasn't a girl anymore, but someone on her way to being a *woman*. Worse now, he knew what it was like to have her, knew the intimate curves of her body, knew how she sounded when he entered her, when she was satisfied and happy, and curved into his arms.

He knew it all, and as much as he thought he had forgotten those details, it was clear they were very much alive in his memory.

He also remembered their breakup, the swift demise of a relationship that had once seemed golden. He'd taken her to Chicago, intending to propose. At the end of the weekend, just as he was about to pull the ring out of his pocket, Jenna had dropped a bombshell.

She wasn't going to college in Indiana. In fact, she wasn't staying in Riverbend one more day. She was moving to New York. She'd tried to talk him into going, too, into attending culinary school in the city. For a while, he'd considered it, then realized all those days of goofing off in high school had caught up with him and his grades weren't good enough for the prestigious culinary institutes. Nor did he have any desire to trade one permanent address for another. He wanted to see the world, and he'd thought Jenna would go with him, or worst case, wait for him to return.

But as he'd watched her pack, he'd realized something. They were headed in different directions. Stockton's dream had always been the same—wander the greatest cities in the world, learning the restaurant trade. Jenna had made it sound as if she wanted the same thing, but all the while, she didn't. She'd been making plans, applying to colleges, looking for apartments. The betrayal had stung.

After all this was over, she'd be leaving him behind again. If he was smart, he'd remember that.

The sauce came together, bubbling up and thickening

with each whisk. Stockton stepped back. "Now add a little nutmeg, taste it and see if it needs anything else."

She ran the nutmeg over a micrograter, watched the dark brown dots fall into the creamy sauce, then took a teaspoon and sampled the béchamel. She smiled. "Perfect." Then she held out the spoon to him. "Taste."

His lips closed over the spoon but he wasn't thinking about the taste of the sauce. He thought of how her lips had been here just a moment before, how if he kissed her, he would taste the béchamel, and so much more. And how incredibly foolish it would be to do that.

"Yeah, it's, uh, fine." He jerked away and got back to work mixing the cheese filling for his manicotti.

The waitstaff hurried in and out of the kitchen, shouting orders, asking questions. Conversing with them gave Stockton an excuse to stay away from Jenna. Across the room, Jenna listened to him talk to the staff, but kept quiet herself and focused on her work. With the sauce done, he had switched her back to basic prep work, which kept her busy chopping and dicing. Stockton stayed by the ovens, checking the roasted chickens and baking bread. Putting Jenna from his mind.

At least, that's what he told himself. But as the rush of orders continued to come in, he found himself right next to her over and over again. "Sorry," he said, as he bumped her hip for the third time that day, trying to reach for a spice on one of the upper shelves. It was as if his body was just looking for ways to contact hers, because he definitely didn't run into Larry, the regular sous chef, this often.

She gave him a quick smile. "No problem."

He plated the order of *bracchiole* and pasta, then slid it under the warming lamp until the waiter came to retrieve the plates. A quick glance at the clipboard running the length of the shelf showed no more pending orders. The dinner rush had passed. That meant it was after nine, and time to begin the clean up from today and some of the prep work for tomorrow.

"Why don't you go home?" he said to Jenna. "The dinner rush is over. There'll be a few more stragglers, but nothing me and the prep cooks can't handle."

She leaned against the counter, and let out a deep breath. The front of her apron was a rainbow of stains from the sauces she'd tended and the space under her eyes was shadowed. "Phew, thank goodness that's over. Is it always this busy?"

"Pretty much."

"I don't know how you keep up. I'm exhausted and all I've done is chop a bunch of vegetables and stir some sauces."

"You did more than that. You were a great help." His gaze skipped over the kitchen, past the mountain of dirty dishes that Paul was running through the automatic dishwasher, then over the stack of folded tablecloths, napkins and fresh silverware two of the waitresses were prepping to carry out to the tables. He turned back to Jenna. "I appreciate it a lot."

Jenna perched a fist on her hip. "Are you admitting I was right?"

"Right about what?"

"That you could use the help, and that having me here would be a good idea."

"Okay, yeah, you were right."

She grinned. "I usually am."

It was a moment of lightness, and one Stockton should take as such. But there was something in him—some masochistic urge to dredge up a past that he wanted only to forget—that had him opening his mouth. "Were you right about us?"

Her mouth opened, closed, opened again. "We were better off apart. We wanted two different things."

"We did. And we still do."

She looked as if she wanted to say something, but instead she nodded. "The proverbial fish and the bird."

"I'd say it was more like a shark and an eagle. One of us had to be in constant motion, hungry for the next challenge—"

"And the other flew away as far as possible."

"I remember that as a mutual decision." One of the waiters came in and tacked an order onto the shelf beside Stockton. He glanced at the slip of paper, then began readying a plate of lasagna. "Don't you?"

"You're right. I should go home. I have a lot to do tomorrow," Jenna said. Her voice held a cold, icy tone.

"Jenna," he said, before he could stop himself.

She turned toward him. "What?"

"Why didn't you wait for me?"

A long, sad smile crossed her face. "Because you were always traveling, Stockton. Not just with airplanes and cars, but with your heart. What's the point in waiting for something that was never going to be mine?" She brushed past him, then left the kitchen. Going, as always, in the opposite direction of him.

He reached for a ladle to add extra sauce to the lasagna. Steam wafted off the baked dish, and a melody of scents emanated from the layers of fluffy pasta, thick cheeses and spicy sausage. He'd always thought of lasagna as a marriage of tastes and flavors that pleased nearly every palate. Sweet, spicy, savory, all together. Stockton drizzled sauce over the dish, realizing as the first drops hit the pasta that he'd accidentally added Bolognese instead of the customer's order of classic red sauce.

He scraped the mistake into the trash, then plated

another slice of lasagna. That was where thinking about the impossible got him—making mistakes and trying to combine two things that would never, ever work.

Aunt Mabel had waited up, even though Jenna had told her twice that it would be a long, late evening. Jenna thought about begging off early, and heading to bed, but found herself craving the company. And maybe, over the mugs of tea Aunt Mabel had set out, Jenna could find some of the answers she needed.

"I talked to Betsy after you left for the restaurant today. I told her to go easy on you." It was as if Aunt Mabel had read her mind. Jenna had thought, spending all these years away from Riverbend, that the town gossip would die down. That people would stop judging her because of her mother's actions. But this afternoon with Betsy had proved differently. She was still Mary Pearson's daughter, and every mistake she made seemed to be compounded by that maternal legacy.

"You didn't have to do that."

Her aunt's wrinkled hand covered hers. "I most certainly did. My dear, you've been through enough. It's time that some people in this town learned to keep their noses on their own faces."

Jenna sighed. "That's never going to happen. You know how small towns are. Always dredging up the past, trying to make it fit with the present."

Aunt Mabel's lips thinned. "What my sister did shouldn't be any reflection on you. Why people insist on putting the two together, I'll never know."

Jenna remembered very little of her mother—she'd been seven when her parents died, and her memories were centered around Christmases and birthdays and long sunny days on the farm. But she remembered her mother's smile,

and for Jenna, who'd been too young to understand what—
or who—was making her mother smile, it had seemed
like maybe things were improving, when really they were
heading on a fast downward spiral. "Why did my mother
do it?"

A long sigh whistled out of Aunt Mabel. "I knew you'd
be asking these questions one day." She toyed with her
mug. "She was unhappy. You knew that."

Jenna nodded.

"I don't know if it was really anyone's fault. I think
she just got married too young and didn't really think it
through. Your father was a good man, but they were more
friends than anything else. And when life started throwing
them lemons—"

"Those were grapefruits, Aunt Mabel." Jenna thought of
all the years of poverty, the times when they had teetered
on the edge of bankruptcy. Jenna had been too young to
understand much more than the fact that every bill caused
a fight among her parents.

"It was enough to test any marriage. For a while, your
mother took a job at the library. The extra money was nice,
I'm sure, but with it came…someone else." Aunt Mabel
sighed. "I know she didn't go out looking for a relationship.
It just…happened."

Happened. Jenna closed her eyes, and when she did, she
was back at that day, sitting in this very kitchen, listening
to her aunt Mabel tell her that she would be staying there
from now on. "If she hadn't met that other man, maybe she
never would have died in that car accident. And my father,
rushing to see her, and going off the road, too. It was all
because she met him, Aunt Mabel. And decided she loved
him more than us."

"That's not the whole story, Jenna. Your mother—"

Jenna threw up her hands. "My mother ruined my life

by what she did, Aunt Mabel. I don't want to hear how I should be more understanding or how she loved her family deep down inside. Because in the end, she made the choices that destroyed everyone."

"Aw, Jenna—" Aunt Mabel's fingers closed over her niece's "—I wish you'd stop writing history in indelible ink. Sometimes there's a lot more gray than black to the stories we hear."

Jenna shook her head, refusing to have this conversation again. "Well, let's just hope that Eunice's birthday bash gives everyone something else to talk about."

Aunt Mabel took a sip of tea, then pursed her lips, as if she wasn't happy with the change in conversation, but would accept it. "I think the party will be fabulous. I'm not worried about that. What I am worried about is—" her gaze met her niece's "—you."

"Me? I'm fine." Jenna crossed to the refrigerator for a snack she didn't want or need. "I'm fine."

Aunt Mabel sighed. "I'd really rather you didn't go back to that city. Why don't you settle down here? You could have a great life here."

"I already have a great life." Jenna moved the mayonnaise to the side, and considered some leftover pudding. The chocolate dish blurred in her vision.

Did she really have such a great life? For years, she'd told herself she loved living in New York. After all, she'd dreamed of nothing else for as long as she could remember. Living in the city, surrounded by the sights, smells, sounds, hundreds of miles from small-town America...that was what she'd thought she wanted.

Until she actually had it and she found herself lying in her bed at night, wishing the traffic would die long enough to give her a taste of the near silence of Riverbend nights. She'd walk the streets, and miss the expansive views of the sky, the fresh scent of a spring breeze. She'd visit the same coffee shop three times in one week, and every time be treated like just one more customer, rather than walking into the deli in downtown Riverbend and hearing someone call out her name, even if she hadn't been there in a month or a year.

But living in Riverbend hadn't been all Utopia, either, and she needed to remember that.

"I have a great life," she repeated. "And when this is over, I'm going back."

Aunt Mabel sighed. "Well, you can't blame me for trying to convince you to stay here and put down some roots."

Jenna shut the refrigerator door and leaned against it. "What roots do I have in this town, Aunt Mabel? Besides you?"

"More than you think, my dear." Aunt Mabel looked as if she wanted to say something more, but didn't.

Jenna withdrew the chocolate pudding from the fridge. She retrieved a spoon from the drawer and returned to the kitchen table. The first bite of pudding hit her palate with a smooth, cold sweetness. Exactly the antidote she needed for the topsy-turvy day she'd had. After a while, she got up, and had a second bowl of pudding, topping it with a squirt of whipped cream.

It had been one of those days. And then some.

CHAPTER SIX

THE COLD AIR HIT STOCKTON like a punch to his jaw. He loved winter, but not when the temperature dipped below zero. He hurried down the sidewalk toward Samantha's bakery, his coat drawn up against his neck, and wondered idly if Rustica would succeed as well in Florida as it had in Indiana. If winter kept its icy grip on Riverbend, he'd be sorely tempted to try a Gulf Coast relocation.

As he rounded the corner, he nearly collided with a tall figure in a thick wool coat. "Jenna."

Surprise lit the notes of his voice. Sure, she'd been here for a few days already, but every time he saw her, it caught him off guard. It had to be because he'd gotten so used to not seeing her. Not because every time they were together she had him asking himself questions he tried never to ask.

"Stockton. What are you doing out in this cold?" The fur-trimmed hood of Jenna's coat concealed her lithe figure, and made her seem more fragile, not that Jenna was ever vulnerable. The wind blew at her, but she didn't seem affected.

"Heading to Samantha's bakery. I wanted to talk to her about orders for next week."

"Oh." She thumbed in the opposite direction. "Listen, I'm on my way to Betsy's for another meeting, but I'm a bit early. Do you want to grab a cup of coffee and talk about the plans for your anniversary party?"

"You don't have to do that, Jenna. If anything, I owe you for working for me last night. I'm sure you have plenty to do with Eunice's party coming up."

"As do you." She cocked her head and studied him. "You know, it's not a crime to ask for help, Stockton."

"I do—" He cut off the sentence. "Okay, maybe I don't. But this time I am asking."

"Why?"

He couldn't tell her the truth. That something had been awakened in him last night when they'd had that moment over the potatoes, and he'd been thinking about it ever since. That he had stayed up late last night, running through a thousand what-ifs, and always, always, coming back to the same destination. She lived a life apart from his, and always would.

"Because I'm terrible at planning parties," he said, and offered her a grin.

"And I'm terrible at white sauces." Her grin echoed his. "All right. Let's get out of this cold, and see what we can come up with."

They headed into the diner, and took seats in a booth in the back. A waitress brought them coffee, and Jenna wrapped her hands around the hot mug. He noticed Jenna was wearing a tailored white button-down shirt with a close-fitted jacket and matching slacks today. He didn't know designers—couldn't have told a Gucci from a garbage bag—but he could tell an expensive cut and fabric when he saw one.

"I had a lot of ideas for your party," Jenna said. "I've spent a lot of time in Rustica lately and I was thinking if—"

"Jenna Pearson?" The voice cut through the diner, sharp and high-pitched. "Mary Pearson's daughter?"

Tension stiffened Jenna's spine. But she planted a smile on her face and turned in her seat. "Mrs. Richardson. So nice to see you again."

Gertrude Richardson. All towns had a woman like her, someone who thought keeping her opinions to herself was a waste of perfectly good opinions. Stockton wondered how old Gertrude was now—she had to be somewhere in her eighties—and wondered if she'd ever slow down on her one-woman crusade to tell people her version of the truth.

Gertrude propped a fist on her hip. "I hear you're in charge of Eunice's birthday party."

"I am."

"Well, consider this my RSVP. I will not be attending."

"I'm sorry to hear that, Mrs. Richardson. I'm sure Eunice will be disappointed."

Gertrude waved a dismissive hand. "Eunice won't care two whits if I'm there or not. I'm staying away out of protest."

"Protest?" Jenna arched a brow. "Of what?"

"Of her letting you, of all people, be in charge. My goodness, you should be ashamed of yourself, coming back to this town and trying to act like you're some uppity businesswoman, going to show us country folk how it's done." The older woman leaned in closer, sending a wave of floral perfume into the space. "I know you, Jenna. Know where you come from, and it's no fancy city."

Fury raged inside of Stockton. He had lived in this town all his life, and never seen anyone think they could treat another townsperson that way. "Mrs. Richardson, where

Jenna comes from or what she wears has nothing to do with the quality of her work."

"I disagree." Gertrude straightened and a haughty look filled her features. "People are where they come from. Why, their roots form the very foundation of who they are."

"My roots are just fine, Mrs. Richardson," Jenna said. Her voice was firm, but Stockton could read Jenna's face. All her life, the whispers of her childhood had followed her around. He couldn't imagine being the constant topic of gossip and knew it had affected her. Maybe in more ways than he had realized.

"You ask me," Stockton said, eyeing Mrs. Richardson, "we all have roots we aren't too proud of or that we wish were attached to a different tree. Wasn't it your granddaddy, Mrs. Richardson, who was arrested for selling moonshine during Prohibition?"

Gertrude's face paled, then reddened. "That's not the same thing."

"I don't know. Back in those days, I think that was quite the scandal. Seems to me, if we all did a little less judging and a lot more understanding, the world would be a better place."

Gertrude drew herself up. "Well, I never," she said, then huffed and puffed and turned away.

After Gertrude had stomped out of the diner, Jenna turned back to Stockton. "Thank you, but you didn't have to stand up for me."

Stockton's gaze met hers across the table. "I think it's about time someone did, Jenna. And told the people of this town that you're not their personal gossip punching bag."

"I'm…" Her voice trailed off. "Okay, maybe I have been."

"I should have said something sooner. Years ago. But

I was young back then and hell, half those women in the quilting club scared the life out of me."

Jenna laughed, the sound sweet music to his ears. "You and me both."

The moment extended between them for another few seconds. Stockton knew he should say something, should jerk them both out of this connection and back to reality, but he didn't.

Finally, Jenna looked at her watch. "Oh, I'm late for my meeting with Betsy. I really hate to say this, but I have to go." She scrambled out of the booth, swinging her tote bag over her shoulder as she did.

Stockton dropped a few bills on the table and followed after her. They both exited at the same time, and the cold slammed into them, hard. "About the anniversary party," he began.

"I can set up another meeting with you later today or maybe early tomorrow. Or—"

He waved her off. "I trust you, Jenna. Do what you think is best."

"You trust me?" Her gaze narrowed.

He nodded and his gaze met hers. The green in her eyes seemed to deepen, become a storm of its own. "I do."

She glanced away for a second, then nibbled on her lower lip. "What are we talking about, Stockton? A party or something else?"

He took another step, and saw her inhale. Her eyes widened. The cold seemed to disappear, replaced by a growing heat deep inside him. Every time he thought he was putting distance between them, he seemed to do the opposite. What was he thinking? He didn't have time for a relationship, especially one he knew would be complicated. "I don't know. Because last I checked, we were over."

She nodded, but the gesture was short, barely a movement.

"Aren't we?"

"What?"

"Over?"

"What does it matter? You live here, and I live in New York."

"Don't dodge the question, Jenna."

Her gaze darted away from his face and she worried her bottom lip again, wearing off her lipstick and revealing her soft pink mouth. "Of course we're over." The words escaped in a frosty cloud.

"Good. I'm glad we have that settled," he said. "Because the last thing I'd want to do is to repeat past mistakes." He was so close, the sweet scent of her perfume filled his senses, and he could see the slight tick of her pulse in her throat. The wind ruffled the fur around her face, danced across her features. The urge to kiss her rose in him, a force so strong, he had to take a step back to resist the desire. "And I suspect neither would you."

Then he said goodbye to her and headed down the sidewalk, before he did something he knew he'd regret.

"You're doing a good job avoiding him," Livia said later that afternoon when Jenna called her friend using the video camera on her laptop. Jenna had a plan for Eunice's party, but thought it wouldn't hurt to get a second opinion. And, she'd wanted someone other than Aunt Mabel to talk to about the confusing rush of emotions she'd been feeling for Stockton. She'd told Livia the whole story—about dating Stockton in high school, breaking up before she went to college and about thinking she was over him—

Until she saw him and realized she wasn't.

"I'm not avoiding anyone. I'm working," Jenna replied. The stack of notes before her was proof of that. So what if she'd barely accomplished anything since returning from her meeting at Betsy's? So what if her mind had been on Stockton, and on the question he'd asked her, the entire time she sat in Betsy's kitschy Christmas-gone-wild parlor? "In fact, I think I should head over to the party store and check out the options for centerpieces. I was thinking of doing different ones for each table, to symbolize the passing of the decades since Eunice was born. Betsy and I discussed the idea earlier today, and she seemed really excited about it." Jenna flipped the pages and turned a series of sketches toward Livia. "An antique tea cup and a string of pearls here, a set of toy Model T cars here and maybe a tiny disco ball and platform heels here."

Livia nodded her approval, her movements made slow and jerky by the internet connection. "What about the menu?"

"I'm working on that, too." If she could call adding "call caterer to work on menu" to her To Do list working on it. So far, all she'd done was a whole lot of thinking about the caterer.

"Sounds like you've got it all under control."

Jenna laughed. "I think so." The only way to get back on top of her business was to make this work. Between Stockton's party and Eunice's event, she had two opportunities to prove her mettle. A flicker of doubt ran through her, but she ignored it. What was *with* her lately? Why did she keep on faltering?

"Good," Livia said. "I have to go. I'll see you in a few days and in the meantime—" Livia grinned "—call that caterer."

Jenna sighed. "Okay. I will."

Livia leaned in close to the computer monitor, as if she could see inside Jenna's thoughts. "Do you still have feelings for him?"

"Of course not." She toyed with the pen, then clicked it off. "Maybe. A little."

"I'd be surprised if you didn't, honestly. For one, from what you've said, he's a hunk, and for another, you two clearly have a history. How long did you guys date?"

"It seemed like we always did." Jenna took a sip of coffee. The hot liquid seared her throat, good and rich and dark. She'd sent the grounds to Aunt Mabel as a Christmas present, because her aunt had complained about the lack of good coffee in the little town. Right now, though, she barely tasted the Kona blend. "I've known Stockton most of my life, and we just…gravitated toward each other. He was my first friend in elementary school, the one who showed me the ropes, sat with me at lunch and made the new girl feel welcome. I don't know when it became something more. It just did."

"High school sweethearts, huh?"

"And elementary school, and middle school." She ran a finger over the rim of the mug, circling the white porcelain again and again. "I guess it was just expected that we'd end up together. By everyone who knew us, by his parents, my aunt and, I guess, by him and I."

"And yet you didn't. Jenna, that happens to millions of high school couples."

"True." She shrugged, but it seemed such a small gesture for a decision that had changed both their lives. "We went away one weekend, and I realized that Stockton wanted a completely different life than I did. I mean, he'd always said he wanted to wander the world and learn how to cook, but I hadn't thought he was serious, you know? I thought he'd hear about my plans for New York, and go with me. But—" she bit her lip "—he didn't want that at all. Heck, I think he was always halfway to the airport in his mind. I couldn't wait for a man who never knew when, or if, he'd return. I had my own dreams and plans. I had told him a hundred times, but I just think he…didn't listen."

Livia laughed. "He's a guy. I think not listening comes with the testosterone."

"Maybe. But to me, this was huge. If he couldn't listen about the big stuff, how could I be sure he'd hear me on the little stuff? So I went to New York."

An understanding smile filled Livia's face. "And thought he'd follow you."

"No, of course not." Jenna worried her bottom lip again, then let out a breath. "Okay, maybe a part of me thought he would."

"And now you're wondering what might have been, had you stayed in Riverbend?"

"What's done is done," Jenna said. But was it? After that moment in the kitchen at Rustica and on the sidewalk today? Was everything as over as she'd thought?

How could five seconds of conversation in the wintery cold with a man she no longer loved leave her so discombobulated? Since she'd gotten back to her aunt's house, she'd done the only sane thing—and thrown herself into the planning of Eunice's party. "I guess I didn't expect to still be affected by being around him."

"Well, if you're not careful, all those moon-eyed meetings with him will start to make people think you're still interested in him."

"I'm not."

"I know. I heard your many and varied protests." Livia

grinned. "What's that Shakespeare quote? 'The lady doth protest too much'?"

"This time it's true," Jenna said. She got to her feet, gathering the remaining paperwork and stuffing it into her tote. "And on that note, I have a caterer to see, and a party to plan."

Mabel Pearson sat at a corner booth in Stockton's restaurant, sipping a cup of tea while she nibbled at a slice of tiramisu. Stockton watched her for a moment from behind the oval window in the kitchen doors, and grinned.

He wasn't fooled, not one bit. He knew Mabel as well as he knew his own aunts. Heck, he'd spent so much time at her house as a child she was practically family to him, and that meant she often acted like family—by delving into his personal life and then telling him what she thought he should do with his life. Stockton chuckled. Clearly, Aunt Mabel had come here to offer her two cents.

Armed with a fresh cup of tea, Stockton left the kitchen and crossed to Mabel. He slid into the seat opposite her, and laid the steaming mug before her. "A refill for you."

Mabel smiled. "How thoughtful. You were always such a nice boy."

"It's all part of the service here."

Mabel pushed her empty cup aside and took a sip from the new one, eyeing Stockton over the rim. "I hear you're catering Eunice's birthday party. She'll be delighted."

"I hope so. But that isn't what you came here for, I suspect."

"Oh, I'm here for the tea. And cake." Mabel took another sip.

"Aunt Mabel," he said, reverting to the familiar term he'd always called her by, the name she'd insisted on after setting a place for him at the dinner table for the third time in a week, "I know my desserts are great, but I don't think you'd brave this cold for a little cake."

"I've been wondering how long it would take a boy your age to gain some sense."

He laughed. "I'm hardly a boy anymore."

"True. But you can still act like one." Mabel forked off a piece of tiramisu and put it in her mouth. Stockton waited, knowing there was more to come after she swallowed. "You know you broke my niece's heart when you and she broke up."

"She's the one that ended it, Aunt Mabel. Not me."

"If you ask me, a woman doesn't end a relationship unless she has a damned good reason."

He arched a brow at the curse. "Well, either way, it's over."

"You know—" she forked off another piece "—for a long time, I was very unhappy with you for letting her get away."

He scowled. "She left. I didn't let anyone get away."

"Then why didn't you go after her?"

It was the one question he had never asked himself. Eight years ago, he had stood in the Indianapolis airport, credit card in hand, staring at the list of departing flights. There'd been one to New York that morning, and one to Italy. He could have chosen New York.

He hadn't.

"Aunt Mabel," Stockton said, as firmly as he could, "maybe once upon a time it seemed like we should end up together, but it's not going to work. Jenna and I tried it, and found out we're beyond wrong for each other."

"Why?"

"We want different things out of life. We always did."

Aunt Mabel pushed her plate aside, then folded her hands on top of each other. "Are you sure about that? Because if you ask me, the Jenna Pearson who left Riverbend, and the one who returned, are two very different women. And the same goes for you." Her older, wiser gaze met his. "Maybe now you two are the people you should have been back then."

CHAPTER SEVEN

JENNA HATED TO ADMIT that Livia had been right. That Jenna had indeed been avoiding Stockton, and the hour or two she'd have to spend with him, discussing his upcoming event and planning the menu for Eunice's party. After all, they'd worked together the other night and never come close to repeating any of their past mistakes. And on the street earlier—he'd come close enough to her to kiss her, and hadn't.

Clearly, he was over her. She was glad. She didn't need to muddle things by getting wrapped up in Stockton again.

Then why did Jenna hesitate before pushing on the door? Why had she spent a little extra time on her hair, her makeup and changed her outfit twice?

She shook off the thoughts of Stockton, and entered Rustica. It took a moment for her eyes to adjust to the dimmer interior of the restaurant. The scent of fresh-baked bread, followed by the sweet scent of chocolate, swept over her as she made her way farther into the restaurant. Soft jazz music played on the sound system, and the waitstaff moved about the room almost soundlessly as they took the last of the lunch orders, refilled drinks and delivered plates. The entire atmosphere of the restaurant was relaxed, but homey, as if someone had filled a single room with the best Italy had to offer.

Truly, Stockton had done an amazing job. The restaurant held the kind of atmosphere that begged you to linger, to have another glass of wine, a little slice of dessert. It was quiet enough to encourage conversation, and dim enough to drop a veil of privacy over each of the tables without making it impossible to see the food.

She headed for the bar, deciding it would be best to wait until the restaurant died down a little and Stockton had a chance to breathe.

"What can I get you?" The bartender, a rotund man with a goatee and a receding hairline, gave her a smile.

"Just a diet soda, please."

"You got it." He filled a glass with ice and soda, then placed it before her and moved down the bar to tend to the other customers.

Jenna glanced at the banner draped over the bar, announcing the one-year anniversary party in a couple of days. Holding it on New Year's Eve was a brilliant move. People would be looking for a venue to bring in the new year at, and Rustica would be one of the only ones in Riverbend. Already, a slew of ideas ran through her head for the party. Something simple, she decided, that wouldn't overpower the atmosphere or the food.

"Just can't stay away, huh?"

She spun around on the seat. Stockton stood beside the bar, his white chef's uniform nearly pristine—unlike her own from last night. "I came by to talk to you about the menu for the party and the ideas I had for your event, but I can wait until you're done serving lunch."

"We're almost finished. And, Larry is finally all recovered from the flu, so he's back at the stove. The kitchen is under control. More or less." Stockton grinned, then put out his hand. "Come on, let's get out of here for a while."

"Are you sure? I don't mind waiting."

"I'm a hundred percent sure. Sometimes whole weeks go by before I realize I've been here since sunrise, and not left until long into the night. That's why I walked to work today instead of driving. I got to see the world a little bit. And now, that little taste of being outside has whetted my appetite for more."

She laughed. "More? But it's snowing."

He retrieved her coat from the stool beside her, then slipped it on her shoulders. "I hear it's the magical kind of snow, though."

"Magical, huh? I don't know about that. More like cold and miserable. But if you want to go for a walk while we talk, I'm all about keeping my vendors happy." Jenna slid her arms into the wool coat, then waited while Stockton retrieved his own.

A moment later, they were outside. The temperature had warmed to just over freezing, enough to allow the snow to fall, but not so cold to make being outdoors unbearable. Jenna was glad she'd opted to change into the jeans she'd bought the other day, and had pulled on a pair of Aunt Mabel's winter boots. If she'd been outside in one of the designer outfits she'd brought with her, she'd be freezing to death, and in those high heels, not able to walk that far. The sidewalks were quiet, with most of Riverbend's residents avoiding the outdoors, and choosing to drive to their destinations instead. The snow fell in thick, fluffy flakes, covering her coat, her hood, the ground. "I haven't been back in this town forever," she said, glancing around the downtown area with its cute little shops and brightly covered awnings, the decorated street poles, the benches waiting for warmer weather. "Nothing's really changed, has it?"

"That's what I love about Riverbend. You can depend on it."

Jenna snorted. "And that's what I hated most."

"You know, sometimes dependability can be a good thing."

She let out a breath, watched it form a frosty cloud. "Maybe it is. And maybe it's just an excuse not to take a chance."

"What do you mean?"

"Nothing. Nothing at all." She'd let that slip without thinking twice. Before she left the house this morning, she'd vowed not to revisit the past with Stockton. She was leaving in a few days. Leaving him behind.

They walked for a while, not saying anything, their hands in their pockets. "Do you remember that spring that was ridiculously warm?"

She nodded. "It was like summer in April."

"Do you remember what we did?"

"Oh, goodness, of course I do." She put a hand to her mouth, covering the laugh. "We skipped school. Ran down to the deli, grabbed some sandwiches and had a picnic in the park."

"And, I might add, caught hell with the principal the next day."

"You did."

"Because I was the one who was failing Algebra—"

"And I was the one with straight A's."

"You were a bad influence on me," he said.

Jenna laughed. "If I remember right, it was your idea to skip school."

"It was indeed. But you could have stopped me."

"What, and miss one of the best days of my life?" She shook her head. "I don't think so."

"Was it?" Stockton asked softly.

"Was it what?"

"One of the best days of your life?"

What was it about him that made her forget her best intentions and say the very thing she didn't want to say? Try as she might to put the past aside, it came roaring back in Technicolor images. Her and Stockton, laughing as they ran out the back of the school building, dashing down to the diner and laughing so hard they could barely place their order. Then grabbing a blanket and heading to the park, setting up a picnic beneath a gracious maple tree with new leaves still curled onto the branches.

He'd held her hand while the warm sun draped over them, and kissed her a hundred times, a thousand. The entire day had been...

Magical.

Today, she was sure, would not be a repeat of that afternoon. A part of her longed to return to that spring afternoon and wondered where she and Stockton would be today if they'd managed to stay together. Would they still be strolling down those park paths, happy and kissing, or would they be walking separate paths, miserable and lonely?

"Yes, Stockton, it was," she said quietly.

"It was for me, too." His voice was tender, edged with a gentleness that surprised her.

She could have caved to that tone, could have continued this reminiscence. She knew where it would lead—she'd already treaded dangerously close to that path in the last couple of days. Instead, she retreated to the safest subject she knew—work. Because in the end, Stockton was still the man who couldn't be tied down too long. Back then, it had been to a desk in school, later to an address. But really, Jenna was sure, it was always about being tied down to her. "Anyway, I wanted to talk to you about your anniversary party—"

He put up a hand. "Stop right there. I already told you I

trust you to do a great job. You know me well enough, and I'm sure whatever you put together will be fabulous."

"You don't want me to run everything by you first?"

He grinned. "Nope. Surprise me, Jenna."

For a second, she was transported back to the days when they'd been dating. She'd told him she wanted to plan a special evening out for them—a sort of trial run at what would later become her career—and Stockton had said the same thing. *Surprise me.*

And she had. Stockton had talked often about wanting to get away for a beach vacation—something neither of them could afford during their high school years—so she brought the beach to him for his birthday that summer. Carting in sand to the patio at his house, adding beach blankets, a CD player with ocean sounds, and even ordering a clambake from a local seafood place. Stockton had been surprised, and touched, and showed his appreciation. Many times over.

If Stockton remembered that night, he didn't mention it. She told herself she was glad.

"Come on, I want to show you something." Stockton motioned to the left, and she followed as they skirted a drugstore and headed down a side street. As they moved away from downtown and emerged into a less densely populated area, Stockton's steps slowed. "Now tell me that isn't magical." He pointed at a spot ahead of them. "And what's more…fun."

They'd emerged at the back of the town park, beside the small pond that had been converted into an outdoor ice skating rink for the season. A dozen or so people circled the pond, their skates making a sharp swish-swish sound with each scrape of the blade. Snow fell onto the skaters and the pond like fat white confetti, and as the skaters passed the fresh flakes, it swirled into fluffy clouds that danced along the ice.

Jenna inhaled the fresh, clean air, scented with nothing but Mother Nature, and held the breath for a long time. She pressed a hand to her chest, closed her eyes and let the snow drop wet kisses on her cheeks. It snowed in New York, it got cold in New York, but never, ever like this. Maybe because the city was so close, everything so compacted, there wasn't any room to breathe or feel that natural world.

Had she ever taken the time to really *be* when she'd lived in Riverbend? Appreciate that tranquility and beauty or had she always been too busy concentrating on escaping small-town life and running from the ugliness she'd encountered to see the beauty this town offered, too? Had she pushed down her happy memories, choosing instead to believe the worst about Riverbend and its people?

"It's...different from what I remember," she said finally.

"Come on," he said, taking her hand and tugging her down the hill.

Even through her gloves, she felt his touch. Heat surged through her veins, and even though she knew she should let go—

She didn't.

"Where are we going?"

Stockton turned to her and grinned. "Ice skating."

She started to sputter a protest, but Stockton silenced it with a finger on her lips. Suddenly, she couldn't breathe, couldn't think.

"Do you remember when we were little, we went ice skating every winter as soon as the ice was hard enough?" he said. "We skated until your aunt came and dragged us off the ice and back home."

The memories came back to her in a rush. Her and

Stockton, the wind in their faces, laughing and speeding around the icy circle. When they'd been little, they'd never noticed the cold. There'd only been the next adventure to try, the next snow pile to climb. "I remember," Jenna said. "And when we were done, Aunt Mabel would fill us with hot cocoa until our bellies sloshed."

He laughed. "That she did." Then he sobered and met her gaze. "We had fun, Jenna, the kind of fun where you don't worry about today, or tomorrow or yesterday. You just *are*. When was the last time you had that kind of fun?"

"The problem with that is that tomorrow always comes, Stockton. The principal calls you down to his office and reminds you to get back on track. The bills come due, and you have no choice but to go back to work."

"All work and no play, Jenna Pearson, can make you grumpy."

"All play and no work can get you in trouble." She turned away from the pond. "Now, about Eunice's party…"

"No. I'm not going to talk about that right now. I might be all grown up and responsible ninety-nine percent of the time, but for today, I want to be that kid I used to be." His blue eyes met hers. "The one you used to be."

The man knew her too well, shared too many memories, and it showed in the way he repeated her own thoughts back at her. The knot of tension in her shoulders that had been a constant companion for the past months seemed to tighten, as if in defiance against his words. She glanced at the ice skaters, at their laughing, happy, cold-reddened faces, then back at Stockton. "I don't think we should."

"I've poured my whole self into that restaurant for the past year, and I know you've done the same with your business. I think—" his gaze returned to the skaters "—if anyone deserves a few moments to just be, it's you and me."

She should have disagreed, should have told him they

were here to discuss business and nothing more. But she didn't.

She just nodded, then headed the rest of the way down the hill with the only man who had ever been able to talk her into doing something completely and totally insane. The only man with whom she'd ever been just Jenna.

And that was a scarier prospect than trying to navigate a frozen pond on two lethally sharp stainless steel blades.

They rented skates from a vendor who had set up shop in a small red shed sitting on the banks of the pond. The snow had dissipated, with the occasional flake drifting on the slight breeze. Crisp, clean air gave a bite to every breath they took.

"I don't know about this," Jenna repeated, lingering on the bank. She gave the ice a dubious look. "I haven't skated in so long, I'll probably fall flat on my face."

Stockton put out his hand to her. "I'll catch you. I promise."

The words were meant to be nothing more than a friendly offer. But for a second, Stockton wondered if Jenna would read more into his sentences.

Of course she wouldn't. They were both mature adults, who knew where things stood between them.

But as her hand slipped into his, and she flashed a trusting smile at him, he realized something. Things were shifting between them, and if he wasn't careful, they'd shift down a path he didn't want to journey.

He'd meant only to show her a good time, to ease the lines of worry etched between her brows. He got the feeling it was becoming something more. Very quickly. Already, he could feel the constricting reins of a relationship. The *expectations*. Something he'd never been good at fulfilling for other people.

Stockton skated backward a few steps as Jenna came onto the ice. She kept her gloved hand in his, fingers curling tightly as she took her first steps. They stayed that way for a while—him moving backward, her skating tentatively toward him.

It was like old times, but with a new, spicier edge brought on by their entry into adulthood. Holding her hand then had been the act of a supportive friend. Holding it now ignited a fire in him, and as her hips swayed with the motion of skating, his thoughts traveled down decidedly adult paths.

They were just skating. Nothing more.

"You've got it," he said, as her movements became more confident.

"That's only because you're holding me up." Jenna laughed. "I'm too old for this."

"If you are, then what about them?" He gestured toward an elderly couple, gliding across the ice, hand in hand. They were smiling and laughing as they moved, clearly enjoying the experience—and each other.

"They're the exception to the rule," Jenna said softly.

"Yeah."

Jenna and him started moving along the ice, sticking to the far outside of the rushing circle of skaters. Some people shot them annoyed glances at their slow movements, but most offered encouraging smiles, a camaraderie that seemed to come part and parcel with small-town life. A few people paused to say hello to Jenna. A few others, Stockton saw, noticed Jenna and began to whisper.

No wonder she wanted to avoid this town. Every time she was here, people wanted to gossip about the real-life scandal in Riverbend. The blatant love affair, which ultimately left an orphan in its wake when her mother tried to run off with the other man. Stockton wanted to go to every single person who was talking behind her back and confront them.

"Don't," she said softly.

"Don't what?"

"I can see it in your face. You want to go over there and set those people straight, like you did with Gertrude."

"They shouldn't do that."

She shrugged. "I'm the town scandal. When I leave, they'll stop."

He eyed the people again, and reined in the urge to do something. Jenna was right. He couldn't battle every person in this town. "You know what they need here?"

"Railings for the bad skaters?" Her light tone said she was glad for the change of subject.

He laughed. "No, though that might work." He glanced down at their still-clasped hands, and thought if there were railings, he'd have no reason to hold her hand. "A coffee and hot chocolate stand. Somebody could really make a killing at that."

"I think a coffee shop in general would do well in Riverbend. A retreat kind of place, with big leather couches and coffee tables and live music in the evenings." Jenna glanced in the direction of town, as if picturing such a place. "There's one down the street from my apartment in New York. I love going there."

"Sounds like a great place."

"It is." Her skates swooshed as she turned to the left. "Why don't you open something like that?"

He laughed. "Me? Rustica keeps me insanely busy. I barely have a life. I couldn't add another business onto that load." He glanced over at her. "Hey, you should do it."

"Me? But I don't even live here anymore."

"You could always move."

Jenna's hand slid out of his and she skated forward,

wobbling a bit as she did. The cold hit her face and reddened her cheeks, made her breath escape in frosty clouds. The heightened color accented her beauty and made Stockton want to wrap her in his arms and warm her up. The silence between them was broken by the laughter of a child, the quiet conversation of a passing couple.

"This is nice," Stockton said. Maybe if he established common ground again with Jenna he could get her to open up, because despite everything, he wondered about what was shadowing her deep green eyes. "I work so many hours at the restaurant that I never get time to do this sort of thing."

"Everybody deserves time off."

"True. But not everybody remembers that, especially when today is busier than yesterday." He swung around her, skating backward so he could face her while they spoke. "When was the last time you took a vacation?"

She snorted. "I could ask you the same thing."

"The month before I opened the restaurant, I spent a week on a beach. The entire experience of finding the location for Rustica, stocking the kitchen, choosing the décor, had reached a boiling point in me and I knew I'd be no good to the place if I didn't take a few days off to just chill."

The mention of the beach made him think back to the night Jenna had set up a mini beach on his patio. He'd been to real beaches a half dozen times since that night—and none of them had been as special as that one.

"Did you go with someone?" Jenna asked.

She didn't look at him when she asked the question and he couldn't read what was going on in her mind. "Do I detect jealousy?"

"Of course not."

He didn't believe that for a second. "You didn't answer my question."

Her gaze returned to his, and the fire he knew so well flamed in her emerald eyes. "And you didn't answer mine," she said.

He bit back a grin. "No, I didn't go with anyone. I went alone."

She nodded, but he thought he detected a flash of a smile on her face. Again he wondered why and whether he was reading something that wasn't really there.

"I haven't taken a vacation since I moved to New York," she said after a while. "I kept meaning to, but the business sucked up all my time."

They were speaking the same language. How odd, he thought, that they'd ended up leading parallel lives, hundreds of miles apart. "And now? Isn't this time in Riverbend a vacation?"

She laughed. "Riverbend is not exactly a prime destination spot."

"Depends on who you talk to. Some people love small Indiana towns in the wintertime."

She arched a brow.

"Okay, maybe not a lot of people, but some. And those who live here love this town."

"Not everyone does."

"Some people used to love it, and maybe if they give it a chance, they'll love it again."

Was he talking about the town? He'd damned well better be, because he didn't want to fall in love with Jenna again, and vice versa. No matter what Aunt Mabel had said, he didn't see a huge change in Jenna. A lot more tension in her shoulders, yes, and stress in the lines of her face, but that could all be because her business was struggling. What he didn't see—what he'd never seen—was a desire in her for the same things it had turned out he wanted. Like a place to call home and put down some roots. They might be leading parallel lives, but they were living them on two different planets—and with two different ultimate goals.

"Are you trying to sell Riverbend to me?" she said.

"You used to like living here."

"I never did, Stockton. I always wanted to leave."

He shook his head, and pivoted until he was beside her again on the ice. "No, you always wanted to run away. That's what you're good at, Jenna, running."

She let out a gust. "Me? You're the runner, Stockton Grisham. The man who couldn't plant his feet in one place for more than five minutes."

"I'm planted here."

"Are you?"

"Of course I am. I have a business, employees who depend on me, customers who—"

"But what about *you,* Stockton? Has that wanderlust gone away? Are you any more ready to settle down now than you were all those years ago?"

"I'm settled, Jenna." But even as he said the words, he wondered how true they were. He lived in a barely decorated house. Spent so much of his day at work he rarely saw the sun. Couldn't remember the last serious relationship he'd had. "But what about you? You come back here, supposedly to plan a party, but there's more involved."

"It's just a party."

He shook his head again. "I know you, Jenna. And I know there's something you're leaving out. I think half the reason you're here is because you're running away from something in New York."

"No." She whispered the denial and looked away fast. Her eyes shimmered, with the cold? Or unshed tears?

What was Jenna hiding? What was bothering her?

Even now, anxiety knotted her shoulders, set in her jaw. He wanted to take it away, to find a way to coax that smile back to her face. "Do you want to talk about it?"

"Maybe I ran away from us all those years ago," she said. "But I only did it because you let me go."

"I asked you to go with me."

"No, Stockton, you didn't." Her gaze met his. "You assumed I'd go with you. And when I didn't, you assumed I'd wait for you. You never once realized that maybe I had my own dreams, and they didn't match yours." She looked off in the distance. "Either way, it doesn't matter. All that was years ago. We can't go back in time."

"No, we can't." He let out a breath. "And maybe it's a good idea if we don't."

In the center of the ice, a group of teenagers formed a line and held hands. The one closest to the center held his position, while the others skated around, creating a whip effect for those on the outside. It was a dangerous, but common, game among kids. Stockton had done it himself more than once. As the kids picked up speed, the farthest child at the end of the line lost his grip and spun off, arms windmilling, feet reaching for traction on the slippery surface.

Stockton glanced over at Jenna. Her gaze was off on the park, not on the ice action.

Just before the kid reached them, Stockton grabbed Jenna, hauled her to him and out of the way. She let out a surprised grunt when she hit his chest, and the skater slipped past them to skid to a stop at the edge.

"Sorry," Stockton said. "Just trying to avoid a collision."

"Thank you." Her face was upturned to his, her cheeks and lips red from the cold. He could almost feel her heart beat against his, even through the thick wool of their coats.

He should let go, push her away, and even better, get off this ice and get back to work. But Jenna was warm in his arms, and all the reasons he kept coming up with for why he should stay away from her seemed a million miles away. He had missed her, and as much as he just said he didn't want to revisit the past, a part of him really did. He reached up, brushed a tendril of hair off her forehead, and watched her eyes widen in surprise at the touch. "What are you running from now?" he asked softly.

She shook her head, and unshed tears shimmered in her emerald gaze. Damn it all. His heart softened, and he bent down, and brushed his lips against hers. A soft kiss, nothing more than one to tell her he was here, if she needed him, despite their past.

She let out a mew, and the soft kiss lingered, until Stockton forgot about being friendly, about keeping this light and casual, and he opened his mouth against hers. She tasted like she always had—sweet as cookies and milk, and yet also something dark and forbidden. Her arms went around his neck, and he crushed her to him, his mouth covering hers, taking all of her that he could get out here in public.

Stockton heard laughter. Conversation. The swish-swish of skates gliding past them. And he came to his senses.

"I'm sorry." He pulled back, and released Jenna. "That shouldn't have happened."

"It was insanity." She brushed at her face, as if trying to erase his kiss. "We were both, uh, probably caught up in the past or something."

"Yeah. I'm sure that was it."

She hadn't wanted him at all. She'd merely been reacting out of some long held memory. "I've had enough of the cold," Stockton said. "Let's get off the ice."

He waited for her, but she didn't even look at him as they skated across the pond and back to the rental shed. Neither of them said anything as they exchanged their skates for their shoes, and slid back into their winter boots.

"I'm sure you need to get back to work. I'll stop by tonight after the dinner rush at Rustica is over," Jenna said, "and we can go over the menu for Eunice's party then."

"It'll be easier for us to talk somewhere quiet. How about I stop over at Aunt Mabel's and come to you? If it's not too late by then."

"That'll be fine. I'm a night owl."

He remembered, and remembered all the late-night conversations they'd had, each of them sneaking a phone into their rooms, or, a few times, when they'd snuck out of their houses and taken a midnight walk. But he didn't say that. "I'll see you then."

Jenna nodded, then strode across the park. They didn't need to meet later; they could have handled their business now. Stockton had time before the restaurant needed him, but he sensed she needed time away from him as much as he needed time away from her. To regroup. To figure out what the hell had just happened.

And how he was going to deal with it the next time he saw her.

CHAPTER EIGHT

JENNA WASHED THE dinner dishes, leaving them to dry in the strainer, then realized she had nothing else left to detract her from having a conversation with Aunt Mabel, who had waited patiently at the kitchen table, pretending to do a crossword puzzle. Jenna stretched her arms over her head, and stifled a yawn. Beneath the table, she flexed her legs. Every muscle in her body ached. Who knew ice skating could be such a workout?

And not just for her arms and legs. Her mind rocketed back to Stockton's kiss, and she touched her lips, reliving the moment. Insanity, that's what that had been. Some kind of rekindling of old feelings that were better left buried.

It wouldn't happen again.

She had already made sure of that. She'd laid out her plans for Eunice's party on the table, along with a notepad and pen, a clear signal when he arrived that they would be talking business and nothing else.

"Are you going to tell me what happened today?" Aunt Mabel said. "You've been awfully quiet ever since you got home."

The old wooden chair let out a creaking protest when Jenna sat down and leaned back. She thought about not telling her aunt anything, then realized half the town had probably seen her skating with Stockton today. If she didn't already know, she'd know before the sun rose tomorrow. "I went ice skating with Stockton."

Aunt Mabel smiled. "Ice skating? You two used to love doing that when you were kids."

"It was his idea, to give us both a little break in the day. He was right. It was really fun until…"

Her aunt waited.

Jenna let out a breath. "Until he kissed me."

"And did you kiss him back?"

"Aunt Mabel!"

"It's a legitimate question, my dear. And don't think I got to be this age without kissing a few boys myself."

Jenna ran a hand through her hair. "I don't know what happened. You know me, I like to have everything under control, all the time, and this whole thing with Stockton is so far out of my control now, I'm not even sure what I'm doing from one minute to the next. I should never have agreed to use him as the caterer."

"Well, perhaps, dear, it's not just Stockton that has you out of sorts. You haven't been yourself in a long time."

"I'll be back at it soon. I've got a plan and everything."

"I know you will be. But I wonder if that's what you really want."

"What do you mean? Of course it is."

Her aunt's gaze softened. "This last year, when we've talked on the phone, you've seemed like…" She paused. "Well, like you're not as happy as you once were."

"I'm fine." Jenna's gaze went to the quartet of cow-shaped canisters on Aunt Mabel's kitchen counter. The containers had been Jenna's mother's—a bridal shower gift ages ago—and one of the many things that had made the journey from the farmhouse in the country to Aunt Mabel's house in Riverbend. After her parents died, Aunt Mabel had wanted to get her niece out of the isolated country farmhouse and into the city so she could have friends and community to help her deal with the tragic loss of both her parents. To make the transition easier, Aunt Mabel had brought along as many of Jenna's childhood home's furnishings and décor as she could, so the new home would feel something like the one she'd had to leave. And, Jenna was sure, so that Mabel could still feel close to the sister she had lost. For that and many other reasons, Jenna loved her Aunt Mabel dearly.

"Okay, maybe not so fine," Jenna admitted, not just to her aunt, but to herself, as well. "I don't know why I'm making all these mistakes. It's like I'm sabotaging my own career."

She thought of all the appointments she'd missed, the dates she'd mis-scheduled, the meetings she'd forgotten. It seemed like her brain had become a sieve, and she hadn't been able to find a way to plug the holes before her business slipped through, too.

"Maybe it's your mind's way of sending a message."

"What message is that?"

"That you made a wrong choice."

Jenna got to her feet, the chair screeching in protest. "I'll be fine. A few good parties and things will go back to normal."

Aunt Mabel heaved a sigh, and got to her feet, too. "Maybe yes, maybe no. And maybe you just need to get quiet and listen to your heart." She placed a hand on her niece's shoulder. "All the answers you need are there, Jenna. You just have to listen for them."

Aunt Mabel headed out of the room and up to bed, leaving behind the truth Jenna had been trying to avoid. She'd heard the same message twice in one day from two different people—when things got tough, or scary, or she just plain didn't like the situation, Jenna Pearson ran.

A soft rapping sounded on the glass of the back door. Stockton, here as promised. The man had terrible timing. He seemed to arrive when she was at her most vulnerable. She should have told him she'd meet him tomorrow, in the light of day, but truly, they were running out of time to plan this party and a professional businesswoman would get her work in order as early as possible.

She opened the door and Stockton came in, stomping snow onto the mat. "I think winter is never leaving," he said, offering her a grin.

He hadn't worn a hat and a fine dusting of snow coated his dark hair. Her hand reached out, fingers flexing, half ready to brush it away, but then she pulled back and reminded herself that she wasn't the woman who did that for him anymore.

"Do you want some coffee?" she said instead.

"That would be great. Decaf if you have it, or I'll never get to sleep."

"No problem." Jenna busied herself filling the coffeepot, avoiding Stockton's gaze. She'd thought time and distance would ease the heat simmering between them, but if anything, the attraction seemed to be building, as if now that her body had had a taste of him, the only thing it could do was want more.

She would serve him coffee, talk about the menu and keep her distance. Even if being near him again had stirred up a hornet's nest in her gut, swarming through her veins. Making her question her resolve before she even fully put it into place.

A moment later, she laid a steaming cup of coffee before him and sat down opposite his seat.

He grinned. "This is familiar."

"What?"

"Sitting at this table." He smoothed a hand over the maple surface, his fingers skipping over the decades of scuffs and scratches. "Late at night. Talking."

"Knowing Aunt Mabel was in the living room, listening for a break in conversation so she could yell at us to stop kissing." As soon as she said the words, she thought about that kiss on the ice, the heat against the cold, and how much she had missed kissing Stockton Grisham, whether it was right or wrong. And yes, she had missed talking to him, having his quiet, calming presence nearby.

Stockton chuckled. "Your aunt was quite the watchdog."

"She always liked you, though."

"There was a time when she didn't." He wrapped his hands around the warm mug, but didn't sip. His face sobered, and after a moment, he looked up and met her gaze. "Back when we were in high school, she once told me she thought we would end up together."

"We did. For a while."

"I think your aunt meant something a little more permanent. And when I went one way and you went another, your aunt crossed me off her favorite people list."

Jenna shifted in her seat, wishing she'd opted to have coffee, too, just to have something to do. She glanced at Stockton's hands—long, defined fingers, strong, broad palms, and her mind traveled back to the afternoon, to his touch against her face when he'd brushed her hair back. Why had he touched her, kissed her, if he was as sure as she was that there was no chance of them getting back together?

And why did everything inside her want him to do it again?

Didn't matter. After this, she was returning to New York,

and Stockton was staying here. Each of them was going back to the lives they'd had before Eunice's party dropped into their laps.

Jenna reached out, hauled the pile of papers and the notepad across the table and clicked on a pen. "Let's, ah, let's discuss the menu."

If Stockton was surprised by the change in topic, he didn't show it. Instead, he pushed his half-empty mug to the side and pulled a slip of paper out of his back pocket. "Eunice and Betsy are simple people," he said, unwittingly echoing Betsy's words from a few days ago. "And if you ask me, the best meals are those they know well." He unfolded the paper, revealing a copy of the restaurant's menu. As he talked, he pointed to items in the entrée listings, dishes that Jenna recognized from her night working the kitchen. "If you want my suggestions, I'd go for the sausage lasagna with a béchamel sauce, the house salad with a balsamic vinaigrette on the side and lots and lots of garlic bread." He grinned. "Eunice orders a basket of bread every Saturday to go with her supper, and makes Betsy trot on down to the restaurant to get it for her."

She pretended his smile didn't still affect her. That when that grin had broken across his features, she hadn't felt a quiver deep in her gut. That she didn't stare at his mouth and wonder if he would kiss her again.

"That all sounds, uh, wonderful," Jenna said, writing down his suggestions on the paper. Not because she might forget but because it gave her something to focus on besides him.

They finalized the rest of the menu, a process that took just a few minutes. Stockton had clearly done this before, and moreover, knew Eunice's favorite meals at Rustica. He proposed a selection of two desserts besides the birthday cake, "because Eunice has a bit of a sweet tooth," and the fried ravioli appetizer, because it was the one meal Eunice ordered without fail, every time she came into Rustica. Already, Jenna could see the tables, the settings, the colors in the room. She'd echo the hues used by Stockton's restaurant and make Eunice feel even more at home.

"I'm not surprised your business is doing so well," Jenna said. "A chef who knows his customers that well can't help but succeed."

"I've lived here so long, everyone in town is almost like family." Stockton leaned forward, and the table that had seemed like a big enough gulf between them five seconds ago suddenly shrank into nothing. "You know, this town isn't so bad. Sure, there are a few bad apples, just as there are anywhere, but if you gave Riverbend a chance, you might find it grows on you."

"That's easy for you to say," Jenna said quietly. "It isn't you, or your family, that they talk about. And no matter what other things people might have done, it was their words that spoke the truth."

He waited until she'd lifted her gaze to his, until he had her full attention. "How long are you going to let those few idiotic people dictate your life?"

She shook her head. The back of her eyes burned but she refused to cry. She didn't want to think about those days again, but it seemed they were determined to push themselves to the surface.

"They blame me," she said quietly. "I was only seven years old, Stockton."

"I know, Jenna, I know."

She could still hear the whispers. She'd been so little, people probably thought she wouldn't know what they were talking about, or understand that she was the topic. "Do you know what someone said to me once in the grocery store? That it was a blessing my mother had died. A blessing. Because she'd caused so much turmoil in every-one's lives."

"There are some people who are too ignorant to have mouths," Stockton said.

"Those people," she said, her voice hoarse, "God, all they did was talk about it every time they saw me. About how tragic it was that the little Pearson girl had lost every-thing. How her mother had been running around with an-other man. How her parents would still be alive if they hadn't had that argument. How—" Her voice caught on a sob and she shook her head.

Stockton reached out, his hand covering hers. His touch held the comfort of a longtime friend, someone who had been there through the good days and the bad, who knew her as well as she knew herself. Holding his hand was like falling into home.

Why had they ever let their friendship go? Had the end really been that bad, that neither of them wanted to hold on as friends?

"Nothing was ever your fault, Jenna," Stockton said. "And the few people who thought that were just stupid."

She shook her head, keeping the tears in check. Barely.

"It wasn't your fault," Stockton repeated. "You must know that."

"I do, but…" She bit her lip. "But other people think differently. They think if my mother had never met that man, never had me, then maybe she wouldn't have been in that accident. And they blame her for my father's death. If she hadn't been hurt, he wouldn't have been rushing to the hospital." She shook her head. "People loved Joe Pearson. Thought he was the salt of the earth, and when he died, it was like they took out their grief on me, because my mother wasn't there to blame anymore."

"People change, Jenna."

Not everyone, she thought, thinking back to the whispers she'd overheard. Sure, there'd been people in town who had offered a helping hand here and there. Some who had donated clothes, others who had dropped off food at Aunt Mabel's. But none of that made up for the whispers. "If I stay here, I'll always be that girl," she said. "And all I ever wanted to do was get away from being her."

Stockton's fingers grasped hers, and his deep blue gaze connected with her own. "You are always going to be Jenna Pearson from Riverbend, Indiana. And if you ask me, that's a good thing. It means you have a history, a heritage and a hell of a lot of people here who would help you—if you'd just learn to ask."

She shook her head. "You love this town. I don't. So stop trying to sell me on how great Riverbend is."

He was quiet, the moment stretching tight between them as a new elastic. "What are you doing tomorrow morning?"

Gratitude washed over her at the change in topic. Clearly, Stockton could see that holding Riverbend up as some Nirvana was never going to work with her. "Picking out decorations for the party. Meeting with the banquet hall to go over the linens and serveware choices—"

He waved off the tasks. "It can wait an hour or two. I want to show you something."

"I shouldn't—"

"You should. I have something I'd like you to see." He grinned. "And no, it doesn't involve ice skating."

Jenna felt an answering smile curve up her face. Stockton had deftly moved the subject area away from disappointments. And back into something that coaxed along the fringes of her better judgment. "If I take any more time off, I won't have a job."

"One morning more, that's all I ask."

Damn, he was tempting. *Everything* about him was a temptation she should avoid because he came with strings, connections. Jenna didn't want or need any of those, especially not in the short window she'd be in town.

She hadn't intended to spend any time at all with Stockton, and she'd ended up cooking with him, ice skating with him, and now, making more plans. She wanted to say no, knew she should say no, but then her gaze strayed to his mouth, to his deep blue eyes that held real concern for someone he'd known for years, and she couldn't seem to voice the right word. "What time?"

"Eight-thirty, on the dot."

"I'll be there," she promised, though she had no idea what she was promising to do. But she had a bad feeling all she was doing was further derailing her plans. They may have gotten the menu planned tonight, but something far more intoxicating was cooking up between Jenna and Stockton.

Something she would put a stop to—at eight-thirty tomorrow morning.

CHAPTER NINE

STOCKTON HALF EXPECTED Jenna not to show up. He let himself into the restaurant a little after eight, drank his fourth cup of coffee of the morning, and waited for the caffeine to take away the sleepless night he'd had last night. He'd tossed and turned for hours, replaying that kiss they'd shared on the ice in his mind, over and over.

Hell, even now, the memory tingled down his spine. Kissing Jenna had been…wonderful. Sweet. Delicious.

It was the aftermath that fit a whole other category of adjectives. He should have thought it through first. Except, when it came to getting involved with Jenna Pearson, smart thinking had never seemed to be part of the equation.

He knew better. And still, he'd gotten wrapped up in her smile, her eyes, her touch. And then last night, he'd been drawn in by her vulnerability. They'd connected in that quiet moment, just like they had in the old days and for a while Stockton had thought they could go back. Be what they were before everything fell apart when she left for New York.

Except, if he was really honest with himself, he'd admit that things between them had been eroding day by day long before Jenna packed her bags. They'd had a lot of fun during those high school years, but they'd never really built anything solid. One big test—and wham, their relationship was over. And he'd chosen the flight to Italy.

If he'd needed a clear-cut sign that they weren't destined to be together, that was it.

Then why did he keep on stirring up a hornet's nest that had been dormant for eight years?

The front door opened, and Jenna walked in, bringing with her a gust of winter. "Good morning." She might as well have been greeting the paperboy for all the warmth in her tone.

Clearly, he wasn't the only one trying to avoid a repeat of what had happened on the ice. And trying to put last night behind them. The best way to do that, he figured, was to get right to the reason he had called her here today. The more he lingered, the more tempting it was to kiss her again.

Stockton grabbed his coat, and motioned to Jenna. "Come on in the back. We have some things to get before we leave."

"Where are we going?"

"To see another side of Riverbend." When she'd said all that about the town last night, his heart had gone out to her. He remembered those days, remembered the people who had talked about Jenna as if she wasn't in the room. Hell, people still talked about the accidents that had claimed her parents' lives, whenever Jenna's name came up. He could understand her wanting to escape the mantle of being "that girl" but she needed to see the whole picture. Remember the other dimensions to Riverbend that existed then, and now.

He held the kitchen door for her, then directed her to take several foil-wrapped containers out of the walk-in refrigerator and put them into a box. She did as he asked, with only a confused glance in his direction. He added a bag of loose dinner rolls, then hefted the box into his arms and headed out the back door, with Jenna right behind him. Stockton loaded the box into the back of his Jeep, then held Jenna's door before coming around to the driver's side and starting the SUV. A few seconds later, they were pulling out of the restaurant's parking lot and heading down Riverbend's main street. The day was clear and crisp, giving the snow still on the ground a hard, crunchy shine.

"Your one-year anniversary party is tomorrow, you know," she said.

"Yep."

"I know I have a lot to finish up for that, and you probably have plenty to do for the meal, not to mention tonight's dinner service. Whatever this is that you want to show me, can surely wait for another day. I hate to take up any more of your time."

"I have time for this," Stockton said. "I always have time for this."

It took about ten minutes to get to their destination, an old ornate church on the corner of the east end of downtown. Stockton parked the Jeep, hopped out and headed for the back of the truck.

He thought she'd be surprised. Ask a few questions. Instead, she sat quietly in the truck and stared at the tall white spire. "They still run that here."

It was a statement, not a question, but he answered it anyway. Still, he was surprised she recognized their destination. Had she been there before? "Yes."

She got out of the truck, and went around to the back, waiting while Stockton opened the door and pulled out the containers. He hefted most of them into his arms, leaving Jenna with one small container and the bag of rolls. She held the door for him as they headed inside the warm, cavernous building.

As soon as the heavy oak door shut behind them, an older, heavy-set man strode down the aisle and toward them. He wore jeans, a black long-sleeved shirt with a white tab at the collar, and a broad, friendly smile.

Stockton balanced the box on one arm and shook the man's hand. "Father Michael, nice to see you again."

"Always good to see you, too," the other man said. He gestured toward the large box filled with several containers of food. "Ah, Stockton, you bless this place so much."

"It's nothing, really." Stockton shrugged, then nodded toward Jenna. "I brought along a friend today." Before he could introduce her, Jenna was stepping forward and wrapping the priest in a warm hug.

"Father Michael. It's been years since I've seen you."

"And I you." He leaned back and gifted her with a smile. "How are you?"

"Fine, just fine."

Father Michael nodded. "I'm glad to hear that. Come, let's bring this food downstairs. We're still serving breakfast, but we can get this stored for lunch and then start service."

As they headed down the aisle and toward a small door at the back of the church, Stockton turned to Jenna. "How do you know Father Michael?" As far as he knew, Jenna wasn't Catholic and he'd never heard her mention attending this church.

"I've been here before."

"To church?"

A small smile whispered across her face. "No. To the soup kitchen. Well, I don't think they called it that back when I was young, but yes, my family has been here." Her gaze drifted over the murals on the walls, the long rows of pews, the velvet tufted kneelers. "I think I told you we were poor."

He nodded. "Your dad's farm struggled, and you had it tough."

"*Tough* doesn't describe it." She let out a long breath. "We had many dinners here, when I was little. Before we left, Father Michael always pulled my parents aside to ask them how they were doing. And if there was ever anything our family needed, it seemed to just appear, without us ever asking."

Father Michael paused, his hand on the knob for the door that led to the basement hall. "I'm glad we were able to do what we could, Jenna. Your parents worked awfully hard out there, bless their hearts. You know farming. It can be a difficult field to make a living. There are times when the harvest is bountiful, and other times when it's…lean."

Jenna's mind rocketed back, to the days in that low-slung white house far from downtown Riverbend. Surrounded by cornfields and to the rear, a herd of cattle that had dwindled more each year. Her father, working so many hours most days she didn't even see him. Her mother, who went gray before she was thirty-five, worrying her days away. There'd been nights when dinner had been nothing more than a thin soup of root vegetables, and mornings when breakfast was a leftover heel of bread. Jenna had been young, and barely noticed anything except a rumbly stomach, but she remembered the worry, the tears, the long, long days without her father.

Was that what had driven her mother, over and over again, into the arms of another man? The constant struggle, the scrabble for the leanest of existences? Had that been enough to turn her from her family and to someone else she thought had loved her?

She could tell from the surprise on Stockton's face that he had thought he knew everything about her. He knew almost everything—except the parts that she had pushed aside, because they were days she didn't want to remember. She didn't say anything more as they went through the side door and down the staircase to the basement of the church. Voices carried up the stairs.

When Jenna reached the bottom step and she took in the people around her—clad in layers and layers of worn clothing, their faces marred by dirt and their smiles filled with gratitude—her heart clenched. "It hasn't changed that much."

"Well, we have new furniture and a bigger kitchen," Father Michael said with a smile, then sobered. "But sadly, no, the need hasn't changed. It's ebbed and flowed over the years, but there are always gaps that the government can't fill. We have a few beds here now, not nearly enough, but still, we try to fill everyone's needs in some way or another," Father Michael said. "Whatever they need, and whenever they need it."

Stockton excused himself from the group and headed over to the tiny kitchen to unload the food he had brought and store it in the refrigerator for later. The rest of the volunteers were busy setting up for breakfast.

"This place has also become a haven for some," Father Michael went on. "A place for others who are down on their luck and need a way to fill their bellies, or their kids'."

A dozen children sat at one table together, others huddled shyly against their parents. A few babies sat in carriers perched on overturned chairs being used as makeshift stands. There was a combined air of desperation and hope hanging in the air. But still, she heard laughter, joking, and saw more smiles than frowns.

She saw herself, so young her feet didn't hit the floor. Her parents on either side of her, urging her to eat more. She remembered a much younger Father Michael, stopping by their table with a kind word for her father, a bag of groceries for her mother. But most of all, she remembered the people, the community that had sprung up here among the neediest of Riverbend.

She glanced at Stockton across the room and he flashed her a quick smile. He'd read her mind, and taken her to the one place that would remind her that there were good people in this town, too. Very good people.

"You were kind to my family," Jenna said to Father Michael.

"Being kind is part of being Christian," he said, laying a comforting hand on her shoulder. Then he smiled. "And speaking of being kind, I better say grace so people can eat."

She chuckled, and watched him walk to the center of the room. As he said grace, Jenna glanced around once more and realized those who were helping—everything from setting up the buffet line to handing out bags filled with what she assumed were toiletries—were people she recognized from town. Samantha's aunt, who often worked with her niece in the bakery. Mrs. Richards, Jenna's third-grade teacher. The husband and wife who lived in the little blue house across the street from Aunt Mabel. So many familiar faces, all working together in their efforts to help the less fortunate.

And not one of them—not the people here to help or the people here who needed help—looked at Jenna Pearson and whispered. Here, she was merely a welcome set of hands.

When the prayer was done, people rose, crossed to the buffet line and began loading up their plates with scrambled eggs, toast, fried potatoes and bacon. Stockton was on the other side of the line, serving eggs with a smile. Jenna slipped into place behind him, donning the apron and latex gloves another volunteer handed her, then took up the tongs for the toast and dispensed slices to the people passing her station. A few who knew her greeted her, asked why she was in town. She kept the conversation simple and the line moving.

This place had filled her when she was hungry, supported her parents when they were in need. Had Stockton been right? Had she purposely forgotten the other side of Riverbend because she'd been too busy nursing a hurt caused by a few bad apples?

"T'ank you," said a little girl in a pink floral jumper that was too short for her skinny frame. She picked up the piece of toast Jenna had just laid on her paper plate and took a big bite, then smiled. "I love toast."

Jenna smiled and added a second piece of toast to the girl's plate. "Me, too."

Her mother rubbed a gentle hand over her daughter's blond locks, then the two of them moved down the line. The woman looked about Jenna's age and Jenna wondered if perhaps she had known her back in school. As the line moved along, Jenna realized several of the people looked familiar, and that fact disturbed her even more. It was so easy to forget, to push aside the signs of those in need.

For so long, she'd been concentrating on her own business, on her own problems, never thinking about the others who had it worse. She'd forgotten that there was a bigger world outside her own, and that world had once supported her, and her family, with food and hugs.

And without judgment.

"Oh, my goodness. Is that you, Jenna Pearson?"

The woman's soft voice seemed to be a blast from the past. Jenna paused in handing out toast and focused on the woman's face. It took a moment before recognition made it past the worn, tired face devoid of makeup, the plain brown hair pulled back into a ponytail, the faded, gray jeans and sweatshirt. "Tammy?"

"Yep, that's me." She waved a hand over her thin frame. "Had a few tough times as you can see, but I'm glad this place is here."

"Me, too," Jenna said, and meant it. For people like Tammy Winchester, for the others in the room, and for her parents, having a refuge like this, even in a town as small as Riverbend, meant no one had to go without a meal.

"Things are looking up, though," Tammy said, as she held her plate toward Stockton so he could add a serving of eggs. "I have a job interview next Tuesday." She smiled. "Wish me luck."

"Really? What are you interviewing for?"

Tammy smiled. "Anything they'll hire me to do. I'm not picky."

In high school, Tammy had been a part of student council, a member of the cheerleading squad, one of those women who had a ready smile all the time. The same smile was there, and Jenna was sure, so were the same talents. "I'm sure you'll do fine. If I remember right, you were the star student on the debate team."

A pleased look filled Tammy's face. "You remember that?"

"Of course. You were the one the rest of the team relied on whenever we needed a quick, smart response." Jenna smiled.

Worry creased Tammy's brow. She picked at the edge of her toast. "Well, it won't matter what I say unless I find something to wear. The church donates clothing items, but there's really not a lot of businesswoman kind of clothes. Know what I mean? I'd love to wow them at this interview." She glanced over her shoulder, saw the line backing up, and gave Jenna a little wave. "Well, I better get going. Talk to you later, Jenna."

"Good luck at your interview." Tammy moved down, and as the line progressed, and Jenna caught snippets of conversations, she realized Father Michael's refuge was doing more than just feeding people. There was discussion about available jobs, tips on writing a resume, a mention of a class to show one woman how to use a computer.

"This is amazing," Jenna said to Stockton as the line dwindled and the workers began cleaning up from the meal. "So much more than what I remembered."

"The reach of this place expands every year," Stockton said. "Father Michael really wants to make it about much more than food. He wants people to see this place as a resource. He and his team help people with everything, from finding affordable apartments to interviewing for a job. There's not a lot of need in a town as small as Riverbend, at least compared to a city, but he makes sure that whatever need there is, it gets met."

Jenna took the leftover toast and began storing it in plastic wrap. She thought of the Stockton she used to know, a boy who had been too concentrated on having fun to ever do anything practical or serious, or sacrificial. And here he was, clearly a regular behind the buffet line, and also a generous donor of food. Food that came from a restaurant he had opened up in this town, yet one more way he'd set down roots and also boosted the local economy. Stockton had changed, she realized, in more ways than one. "Why are you here?"

"Because it makes me feel good. I'm sure it would be easier to let the leftover food go to waste, but this is rewarding. I found something here," he said, pausing as he loaded the empty chafing dish into the sink, "something that I hadn't realized I'd been looking for until I came across it."

Yes, Stockton had changed—become calmer, more centered. A man who knew what he wanted, and even more, had it.

She envied that peace. For as long as she could remember, she had felt a constant churning in her gut. She'd called it need for a change of her life, and for a while there in New York, the churning had been quieted by success. But then over the past few months, heck, maybe Aunt Mabel was right and it had been more than a year, the churning had returned, becoming a full-blown whirlpool threatening to take her down into its vortex.

And so she had begun to screw up. At first, she had attributed it to her business growing too fast, being too busy to mind the details, but was there more to her actions, as her aunt had said? Was it some subconscious fight to find what Stockton clearly had?

"What did you find here?" she asked Stockton. Maybe if she knew, she'd understand better and be able to find the same.

He thought a moment. Beside them, soap bubbles popped and disappeared in the hot dishwater. The bustle of the kitchen cleanup continued, and out at the dining tables, the low, happy hum of conversation rolled. "That when we help other people, it reminds us of the goodness in others, and in ourselves. And reminds us that there is good everywhere, including this town."

Jenna's gaze took in the people in the room, their faces content, filled by more than just a meal. "You're right," she said softly. "I guess I got too wrapped up in the bad to focus on the good. It was easier, I guess, that way."

Stockton stopped cleaning for a moment, and met her gaze. "I think people do that a lot. About more than just what's happening behind closed doors—about themselves and who they really are."

Jenna loaded the last of the dishes into the dishwasher and thought about Stockton's words. She'd come here with him this morning, sure she'd prove him wrong. Sure she'd find one more argument in the case against Riverbend. Instead, she'd been reminded that this town did, as Stockton said, have another side. One that helped without judging, without asking anything in return. A side that had helped first her family, and later her, when she'd needed it.

She'd returned to Riverbend, so sure this town could never grow on her again. Confident that Stockton Grisham hadn't changed at all. After today, she could no longer deny the truth—

She'd been wrong. There was only one person she didn't really know anymore.

Herself.

CHAPTER TEN

"Don't tell me that's what you're wearing tonight."

Jenna turned, the simple black dress she'd been considering pressed to her chest. "I might. If I even go."

"It's New Year's Eve, Jenna. You have to go out, it's a tradition. And you have to look sexy. That's a rule." Livia grinned. Her plane had arrived that afternoon, and in the few hours since, Jenna had caught her friend and former employee up on all the party plans. Not so much on the personal events. Jenna's mind was still processing how Stockton had surprised her in the past few days.

Livia entered the room and took a seat on the quilted comforter. "Aren't you supposed to go? I mean, you planned this party."

"I'm sure Stockton will have it all under control." Jenna draped the black sheath dress over the chair beside the vanity she'd sat at for so many years, it seemed like it was part of her. The scarred white furniture had been one of the first things Aunt Mabel bought her when they moved to the house in the city, and the first time Jenna had ever owned a matched bedroom set. Even though she'd long ago outgrown the scalloped edged pieces with their painted on pink flowers, she loved every bit of it, from the twin bed to the long, low dresser.

"Maybe. Maybe not. Either way, you should go, if only

to have an excuse to wear a great dress." Livia picked up a second dress lying on the bed. The red jersey fabric hugged Jenna's curves, while the low V-neck offered a tantalizing glimpse of what lay beneath. When Jenna had packed it, she'd been sure it was a waste of valuable suitcase space, but now she wondered if maybe Livia had a point.

How would Stockton react if she walked into the room, wearing this dress? Would he smile and take her in his arms? Or would he be so wrapped up in his party that he barely even noticed her presence?

She glanced at her luggage. In a few days, she'd be packing and heading back to New York. And Stockton would once again be a piece of her past. He had changed in many ways, but not in the ways that were most fundamental to a relationship. He'd danced around them being together again, but hadn't done anything more than that. Just like in years past, Stockton had one foot toward the door even as he said he wanted to stay.

She sighed. "I have so much to do for Eunice's birthday party that I don't really have time to go out tonight. I already made sure the restaurant was all set up for the party tonight. I don't have to be there to host it." She rehung the dress in the closet, then reached for her robe.

"It's New Year's Eve," Livia said, retrieving the red dress and pressing it into Jenna's hands. "A time for new beginnings." She closed Jenna's hands over the plastic hanger. "And if anyone needs a new beginning, it's you."

"I don't—"

"You do. You've been in this rut for too long, Jenna. Get out tonight, have some fun. And maybe you'll find what it is you've been searching for."

Was that why she had returned to Riverbend? She'd been searching for something, something to fill that yawning hole in her life?

Jenna took the dress and turned toward the mirror, holding the crimson dress to her chest. She flipped her black hair over her shoulders, giving her a preview of how she'd look. "And what do I do when I find it?"

Livia smiled, and pressed her cheek to Jenna's. "Grab it with both hands. And never let go."

A local oldies band was setting up on the temporary stage erected by the bar. In the center of Rustica hung a glittery strobe light on a retractable chain, waiting to be lowered at midnight. Streamers shouting "Happy New Year!" and "Happy Anniversary, Rustica!" hung from one end of the restaurant to the other, while hundreds of silver and white helium balloons bobbed along the ceiling. The decorations were classy and echoed the festive, hopeful mood Stockton had wanted for this combination anniversary/New Year's Eve party.

It was exactly what he'd envisioned. He should have been thrilled. Instead, a nagging sense that he was missing something hung heavy on his spirits.

A buffet of dinner selections had been set up along one wall, an appetizer station along the other, and in the center of Rustica—a massive cake baked by Samantha and offering congratulations on a first year's success. All the staff had arrived for the evening—some grumbling about working New Year's Eve, but most happy to be there to celebrate the momentous occasion. Everything was perfect—and hopefully would be well enjoyed by the hundreds of people who had RSVP'd to the party invitation.

Jenna had outdone herself. She'd created a fun environment, but not one that overshadowed the restaurant itself. He knew when he put the party in her hands that everything would be taken care of, and in a way that defied his expectations—not to mention anything he could have put together. The only thing he had to worry about was the food, and even that had Jenna's thoughtful touch. He glanced at the hand-lettered signs posted along the buffet line: AULD LANG SYNE MINESTRONE; CELEBRATION CONCHIGLIEI; NEW BEGINNINGS ANTIPASTO.

It was clever, without being cutesy. He'd been right to trust her with the party, to simply hand over the reins and let her do her job.

Stockton straightened his tie. Damned thing felt like it was going to strangle him. No wonder he never wore the stupid things. He was far more comfortable in the white cotton chef's shirt, or a simple T-shirt and jeans, and being behind the stove instead of on display. But tonight he was spending his time in the front of the house, greeting his guests and thanking each of them for the business. Without these customers, he wouldn't be where he was today—standing in the center of his own restaurant, enjoying the success he had always dreamed of having.

He thought of his father, and wondered if there would ever come a day when Hank Grisham would sample his son's success. Stockton had called Hank the day he opened Rustica, and a couple of times since, and although his father had congratulated him, he'd held firm to the belief that no one could make a successful restaurant in the town Hank had seen as a little pocket of hell.

Stockton glanced around the room again and wondered if perhaps it was more that his father didn't want to admit that his son had done what he himself had never been able to do. Before Stockton was born, Hank had toyed with the idea of a restaurant in Riverbend, even went to work at one in a nearby town to learn the business from the inside out. But when that restaurant failed, Hank had given up on small towns, and pretty much given up on his marriage, and headed out on a cross-country, then cross-world journey with his knife and apron.

Stockton knew he *should* be enjoying his success, celebrating a great year in business. But the emptiness that had plagued him in recent weeks returned with a roar. He told himself it was merely the inevitable letdown that came with reaching a milestone.

Yeah, right.

Nine o'clock arrived. Stockton opened the restaurant's doors, cued the band and started the party. For the next two and a half hours, he was able to forget the emptiness, and concentrate on his customers. Still, his concentration was a fragile thread, and after the twelfth time he glanced toward the door, he knew why.

Jenna.

She hadn't come to the party. Why?

A little before midnight, the front door opened, and Stockton's heart leapt, then dropped again when he realized it was only Betsy and Earl stopping by. "The place looks great," Earl said. "Where's the food?"

Stockton laughed, and gestured toward the buffet tables. "Already have a plate with your name on it over there, Earl."

Earl grinned and rubbed his belly. "Glad to hear that, Stockton. Your cooking is the best—" he glanced at Betsy who shot him a warning glare "—the best, second to Betsy's, of course."

Betsy gave him a tender pat on the shoulder, then turned back to Stockton. "You've done a good job," she said. "I think these decorations are wonderful."

"It wasn't me. This was all Jenna's doing."

Betsy glanced around the room again, reassessing the décor. "Well. She did a mighty fine job. Let's hope she'll do just as good a one with my sister's party."

"She will. You can count on her." Though as he said the words, and watched Betsy and Earl cross to the buffet, he found himself glancing at the door again.

He was about to turn away when he saw a familiar pair of green eyes framed by soft ebony curls behind the glass. *Jenna*.

She entered the restaurant, at first not seeing him, but rather looking past him as her gaze scanned the crowd. Another woman stood beside her, a tall blonde in a blue dress. Her friend Livia, Stockton guessed, the one arriving today. Livia whispered something to Jenna, then headed down the stairs and over to the bar. Stockton waited, and watched, as Jenna's gaze swept around, then came back to center.

To him.

A smile broke across her face as bright and sweet as spring sunshine. He felt something stir deep inside his gut, and wondered what it would take to keep that smile permanently on her face. Wondered what it would be like to see that smile every single day.

The year was starting anew. Maybe they could, too.

"Hi," she said, the word soft and quiet amid the noise of the full restaurant.

"Hi." Stockton took two steps forward. For some reason, he felt nervous and awkward, like he was a teenager again. "Let me, uh, take your coat."

She grinned. "You're not in the kitchen tonight?"

"Nope. Tonight I'm part of the…entertainment." He chuckled. "Though some people might ask for their money back after they spend enough time with a chef who would rather be in the kitchen than playing the small-talk game."

"Oh, I doubt that."

"I have to thank you," Stockton said. "The restaurant

looks incredible. When I walked in here today, I hardly recognized the place."

A flush filled her cheeks. "I should be thanking you. It's not often that I have a client just hand over the keys and say he trusts me."

"I do trust you, Jenna."

She shook her head, as if trying to head off words she didn't want to hear. "I'm glad you're pleased with the results. Anyway, I just came by to check on things and make sure it all went off without a hitch." She started to button her coat again, but Stockton put a hand on hers.

"Stay. Enjoy the fruits of your labor. Have some pasta and sauce. I think that might be a bit more appetizing than your aunt's black-eyed peas and lentils."

Jenna laughed. "How'd you know she's got those ready?"

"I know your aunt Mabel, and if there's one person who's got superstition down to an art form, it's her."

"When I left, she had a broom beside the back door. Said she was going to stay up until midnight, then sweep all the bad luck out the door. And she's also one of the reasons I'm wearing red." She let her hand fall away, and the coat fell open, revealing a red dress that hugged her curves. An incredible, stop-his-heart-for-a-second dress. Holy cow.

"You look great in that color," Stockton said. Understatement, he realized. She looked amazing.

"Thanks. Though I'll have you know, Aunt Mabel's superstitions extend beyond dresses and into underwear." Jenna leaned forward and her voice dropped to a whisper. "She wouldn't let me leave the house unless I was wearing *all* red."

A surge ran through him, and his mind pictured what surprises might be beneath the red dress. Holy cow times ten. For a second, he imagine himself unzipping the dress, watching it fall to the floor, revealing the scraps of red beneath. "You're wearing red underwear, too?"

The flush returned to her cheeks. "I can't believe I told you that. I just…well…"

"We used to tell each other everything," he finished for her. Then he quirked a grin at her. "Hey, anytime you want to tell me about what's under your dress, I'm all ears."

Jenna swatted him, and in that moment, Stockton could believe they were back to how they used to be, years ago. He wanted to hold on to this moment, bottle it, and bring it out after Jenna had left.

"Your aunt's led a pretty charmed life," Stockton said. "Maybe there's something to all that superstition stuff."

"Maybe." Her gaze connected with his. "And…maybe I can stay for a little while."

"That'd be nice," he said softly.

She slipped off her coat. Stockton's gaze drifted down her lithe frame, over the V-necked red dress, past her trim waist, lingering on her bare legs, enhanced by strappy red heels. Desire surged in his veins, pounded in his head, compounded every time he looked at her lips and thought about what she'd feel like in his arms again.

Damn. This was dangerous.

He should turn around, go back to the party and stop letting himself get wrapped up with this woman. Instead, he took her winter jacket, handed it to the coat-room attendant, then put out his hand. "Do you want to dance?"

She hesitated, and for a second he thought she'd say no, but then the smile curved across her face again, and she nodded. "Though I warn you, I'm no Ginger Rogers."

He chuckled. "That's okay. My dancing skills are pretty much limited to slow dances. Anything else, and I look like a chicken flopping on the floor."

"I remember. You were my prom date."

He groaned. "I still can't believe you let me wear that light blue tux."

"It wasn't so bad, Stockton." A soft smile filled her face, and again he got the feeling that if they could somehow hold on to this moment, everything would be okay between them.

"Do we dare a repeat?" he asked.

"Yes. We do." Her hand slipped into his as they threaded their way through the crowd and onto the small dance floor set up to the right of the bar. As they reached the parquet, the band segued from the fast pop song they'd been playing to a slow country ballad. "Did you plan that?" Jenna asked.

"I wish I was that clever, but no, I didn't." He put out his arm, and she stepped into the space, then he took her opposite hand, and they began to step to the side, their bodies not quite touching, but close, very, very close. "Do you remember our first dance?"

She nodded. "Eighth grade. We were all pimples and gangly bodies, and for half the dance all the boys hugged the walls—"

"Too nervous to talk to the girls." He shook his head at the memory. "I sat beside you for seven years in school, and talked to you every day, but you add in some music and dimmed lights, and I was as nervous as an actor before the curtain rises."

"And are you nervous now?"

"Hell, yes."

She laughed. "Good. Because I am, too."

"Don't be nervous, Jenna. It's just me." He brought his face closer to her hair, inhaling the light vanilla-cinnamon fragrance. For a moment, he was lost, in the feel of Jenna in his arms, the scent of her teasing his senses. His gaze drifted along her delicate jaw line, and his body tensed as the desire to kiss her there, to trail kisses all the way down her body, rose inside him. His mouth hovered over her skin, so close his breath made little paths in the fine hairs along her neck. He pressed Jenna closer, until her body and his merged, their steps becoming one and the same. He ran a hand down her back, the dress hitching a little with his touch.

"What are we doing?" Jenna whispered. He could feel the words against his shoulder, and more, feel her tremble as she spoke them.

"I don't know."

It was the truth. He didn't know what he was doing. Or why. All he knew was the sound of this insistent need, pounding inside him, telling him he couldn't let her get away again. Even as he knew they hadn't settled a thing, and as far as he knew, the life she wanted was the same one she'd wanted when they'd broken up.

One that would not include him.

"We shouldn't..." she said, but didn't finish the sentence.

"We've already made this mistake," he said, and still his lips hovered over her neck, and the pounding kept pace with his heartbeat.

"Yeah," Jenna said, then she turned her head just enough so that her mouth was under his.

The band had stopped playing, and around him, the sound of cheering and counting finally infiltrated Stockton's brain. Midnight—they'd reached midnight and everyone was counting down those last few seconds. A sense of magic filled the air, highlighted by the shiny decorations, the sparkling confetti littering the tables. It seemed, at that moment, as if anything was possible.

As if anything he wanted could be his.

The crowd laughed, glasses raised, an air of happy

anticipation filling the room, but still Stockton's attention was riveted on Jenna. Her mouth, her touch. Simply… her.

People chanted the numbers together. "Ten…nine… eight…"

"We could get hurt again," he said.

"Five…four…three…"

"Very hurt," she whispered, and her gaze locked on his. The heat that had been building between them reached a fever pitch. His gut tightened with desire, and he realized that the most magical thing in the room was Jenna.

"Two…one…Happy New Year!" Cheers erupted around them, horns blew, glasses clinked and the band launched into "Auld Lang Syne."

They were old acquaintances, just as the song said, and if they were really honest with each other, they'd admit the truth. They'd never forgotten, not for a moment. And right now, all Stockton wanted to do was remember her, remember this.

"Happy New Year, Jenna," Stockton whispered, then he closed the gap between them and kissed her.

Jenna melted into Stockton's arms, her resistance gone the second he'd lowered his lips to hers. Heck, she'd been unable to resist that man from the day she met him. She'd always been attracted to Stockton, truth be told.

And kissing a man who had known her as long as Stockton had meant he knew every nuance of her mouth, every touch that would drive her wild. His lips claimed hers with a heat that built and built, a sweetness flavored by reunion and second chances. His hands ranged up and down her back, playing a tune that only he knew.

Electricity charged her body, and she leaned into him, craving more of his touch, his kiss, simply craving him. Her mind emptied of every thought except the feel of Stockton against her. He tasted of coffee and red wine, like a special dessert just for her. His tongue swept inside her mouth, and she echoed the gesture, dancing with him. A groan built in her throat and escaped in a soft mew. "Stockton."

He drew back, pressing his cheek to her hair. The tender move nearly brought her to tears. "Aw, Jenna, I've missed you."

She shook her head, and backed up. "We can't do this. I'm going back to New York, and you're staying here."

He caught her hand. "Stay. Don't leave. You can run a business here as easily as there."

"I can't, Stockton. You don't understand. I'd never be happy here."

"Because you hate Riverbend so much or because you never allowed yourself to love it?"

"I…I can't do this." *Can't answer your question. Can't stand here and fall for you all over again.* Jenna spun away before Stockton could stop her.

And before he could see the tears forcing their way to the surface.

The red dress hadn't brought her luck at all. In the end, all Aunt Mabel's superstitions had done was turn her into a bigger fool than she already was. And raised her hopes for a new-year beginning that was impossible to have.

CHAPTER ELEVEN

"YOU'VE DONE MY FAMILY PROUD," Betsy Williams said. She spun a slow circle in the middle of the Riverbend Banquet Hall and beamed. The room wasn't entirely done— the finishing touches would come tomorrow, shortly before the party—but Livia and Jenna had made a good start on the setup, thanks to Livia's persuasive abilities with the owner of the venue. Jenna was pretty sure Edward Graham had given them the extra day just to score some brownie points with Livia, whom he seemed to have taken a liking to, but whatever the reason, the bonus hours made for a much more relaxed party-planning experience, something Jenna rarely had.

It had been five days since New Year's Eve. Five days where Jenna avoided Rustica and Stockton, and concentrated solely on Eunice's party. There'd been hundreds of photos to sift through for the memory display, and Jenna had let that task consume her. Rather than deal with what had happened on that dance floor and Stockton's repeated attempts to contact her and explain.

Every time she refused to take his call, Aunt Mabel got this pained look on her face and shook her head. Livia had tried to broach the subject twice—and gotten nowhere. Stockton wanted the impossible out of her.

He wanted her to stay in Riverbend. And trust that the

man who had never been able to commit to her was serious about a commitment now. She knew Stockton—too well—and knew better than to put her faith in the impossible.

"Isn't this just amazing, Earl?" Betsy said, drawing Jenna's attention back to the hall. "It's like something out of a TV show."

"It's something, all right." Earl scowled. "Something fancy."

Betsy slugged him. "Now, Earl, it won't hurt you to put on a tie and your best shirt."

"I'm wearing my best shirt." He patted his Mechanics Know How to Make It Work T-shirt.

"You will not wear that filthy thing to my sister's birthday party. I bought you a nice button-down. You'll look handsome."

"More like a man going to his execution," Earl mumbled.

Betsy rolled her eyes, but bit back any additional comments about Earl's attire. "I'm going home to wrap Eunice's present and get the bed-and-breakfast ready for all her relatives that are arriving today. Lordy, it's going to be busy at my place. I'll see you at the party tomorrow. Me and Earl." She patted Jenna on the back. "I never should have doubted you." She held Jenna's gaze for a long time. "I'm sorry."

Warmth spread through Jenna. "Thank you. That means a lot."

Betsy headed out of the building, oohing and aaahing over the decorations as she left. Earl stayed behind, twirling his ball cap in his hands. "I seen your face earlier," he said to Jenna when the door shut.

Jenna bent over to straighten a display of photographs from Eunice's childhood. "What about my face?"

"Every time my Betsy calls you a local, you look like you want to run off the closest cliff."

Jenna laughed. "Considering we're in one of the flattest states in the nation, I'd say that's pretty hard to do."

"You know what I mean, Jenna Pearson, and don't pretend you don't." He wagged a finger at her. "I've known you all your life. Why, you used to sit in my garage on that stool I got, and watch me work on your father's truck. You'd hand me a wrench when I asked for a screwdriver, and be just a general pain in the neck, like most kids are, but…" He shrugged and his gaze dropped to the floor. "I didn't mind much."

"I remember that. The smell of the oil, the country music you were always playing."

"Nothing can make the day go by faster than a little Travis Tritt." Earl grinned, then sobered. "And I remember when you came to live with your aunt Mabel. After your parents were gone, she moved you on into town, and brought you up right."

"My aunt's a wonderful woman." Jenna switched one frame for another, then shifted another a little to the right, perfecting the display.

Earl nodded. "Yep, she is. Quite the woman." He twirled the ball cap some more. "So was your momma."

"She was a good mother," Jenna said. "Who didn't always make good choices."

"No, I reckon she didn't. But in the end she did the right thing." He ran his thumb along the ball cap's brim. "That man, he asked her to run off with him. Your momma turned him down flat. Made him madder than a hornet, let me tell you. He was in my shop, getting some new tires before he blew out of town, spouting off like Old Faithful." Earl leaned in closer. "She told that so-and-so that her family was more important to her than any plans he had. That she'd been a fool, and she was staying right here to make things work."

"But I thought—"

"What you thought is wrong. Bunch of nonsense made up by people who didn't know any better. I think that day—" his face softened and his voice lowered "—that day we lost your momma and your daddy, your momma had decided to make her marriage work. She was here in town, picking up wine and flowers and all kinds of romantic notions. People say it was for him, but I know better. That man was long gone, off to ruin someone else's life. Your momma was headed home that day, Jenna. *Home*."

She thought of the intersection where the accident had happened. It was one of those where you could go either way—toward the farm or toward another city. Everyone had assumed that Mary had been going away from the farm, from her family. But what if Earl was right, and she had been going home?

All these years, Aunt Mabel had been trying to tell her that there was more to the story than what Jenna had heard from the gossips, but Jenna hadn't wanted to hear it. She'd simply believed the worst about her mother, because she'd felt so betrayed, so hurt. Sure that her mother was leaving not just Joe Pearson, but her own daughter, too.

"I hated her," Jenna said softly.

"Your life turned upside down. You're allowed a little anger."

"But I should have understood, I should have—"

"Jenna, you were, what, seven when your parents died? Ain't no kid I know that age who can make sense out of the whys and wherefores of the stupid things adults do. Sometimes, you just need a little time to see the whole picture."

"And there were so many people telling me only the worst."

"Don't you listen to people talk," Earl said. "They don't know your mother like you know her. You make up your own mind about her, and you shut those other busybodies out."

"I barely remember my parents."

Earl smiled. "You come over to my garage sometime. Sit on the stool, and hand me the wrench when I need it, and I'll tell you all about him."

Gratitude flooded Jenna, and she reached for Earl, giving his hand a squeeze. "Thank you, Earl."

He shrugged, crimson spotting his cheeks. "You know me, I like to talk." He glanced at the clock. "I have to get going back to the garage. Got a dead Taurus sitting on my lift that needs a new alternator."

"Thanks again. I guess I forgot that there were people like you in this town."

"I ain't nobody but a good neighbor, and you've always had plenty of those."

She thought back, to when she was a child, after her parents had died. She'd been so poor, with so few belongings, and then one day, bags and bags of clothing and toys had arrived on Aunt Mabel's doorstep. "That clothing drive. I remember that. No one ever told us who did that."

"It was Betsy. She ain't never had no kids of her own, and I guess she just thought you were one she could kinda adopt, know what I mean?"

"*Betsy* did that? But I thought…"

Earl waved off her sentence. "Betsy's nicer than she'd like people to think."

And then Jenna remembered. Betsy calling Jenna over when she was riding by on her bike, giving her a stern lecture about road safety. But it had always been followed by a peanut butter cookie. The meals she used to dread at the bed-and-breakfast—Betsy had invited them over at least once a week—and leaving with armloads of leftovers. Abrasive Betsy doing her best to help her neighbor. "That was so nice of her."

"Yeah, well, don't tell her I told you. It'll spoil her reputation. I know my Betsy's got an ornery streak sometimes, but at heart, she's just a protective old goat." He chuckled. "And Pauline Detrich, God rest her soul, she was the principal at Riverbend Elementary, and she used to tell me she'd stop by every day in your classroom and make sure you were catching up to the other kids."

Jenna remembered the older woman making appearances in her classroom, but had never known why. She'd thought it was because the principal was friends with her teacher, or had been sent by Aunt Mabel to check on Jenna. "She's the reason I got in that special tutoring program."

Earl nodded. "You needed a little TLC when you were a kid, and there were plenty of people here who made sure you got it. And your aunt, well, she had it tough, too. Not a lot of money, and a kid she had to feed and clothe. People stepped in, Jenna. Brought you just what you needed, when you needed it."

It was almost the same words she'd heard Father Michael use the other day. All these years, she'd concentrated only on the negative experiences in this town, using them to fuel her leaving when she'd graduated. How easy it was, she realized, to do that instead of think of the good in the people around her.

"This is a town that takes care of its own," Earl said. "And you were always one of its own, regardless of what a few idiots without a stop sign for their mouths ever said." Earl lay a hand on her shoulder. "I've been watching you since you came back here. You've been lost, I think, and coming home, you've been found again. You just don't know it yet. This place is home for you, Jenna Pearson. It always was." Then he left, leaving Jenna alone in the banquet hall, surrounded by pictures of a woman who had spent a hundred years in this very town.

Jenna wandered the hall, for the first time really studying the pictures of Eunice. There were tiny black-and-whites from when she was a child, standing on the front stoop of a low-slung bungalow-style house, eating an ice cream at the summer fair, standing in the woods beside the Christmas tree her father had just cut down. And then, later in her life, pictures of Eunice doing charity work for the local church, accepting a blue ribbon at the pie table, serving hot cocoa at the Winterfest. Happy memories, every one of them.

It wasn't Eunice that left an impression on Jenna. It was the people around her. Members of the town where she had lived nearly all her life. For years, she'd been telling herself that she didn't belong here, that she wasn't a small-town girl at all.

And yet, Riverbend had been there for her, in more ways than she could count. The thought warmed her heart, and made her wonder if she could ever repay that kindness.

She tried to concentrate on finishing the centerpieces, and gave up. Her mind was racing, hundreds of thoughts from the past two weeks crowding her. She grabbed her coat, and headed out the door of the hall, just as Livia was coming in.

"Hey, where you going in such a rush?"

"I just need some air."

Concern knitted Livia's brows together. "Are you okay?"

"Yes." Jenna paused. "No. I just need a little time to think."

"Okay, sure. But if you want to talk, I'm here."

"Thanks, Livia." Jenna drew her friend into a tight hug, then headed out into the bright sunshine. The winter storms had finally passed, and the temperatures were edging into the high thirties. After the cold of the past few days, it almost felt like a heat wave. The snow had turned to slush, forming gray puddles on the sidewalks.

Jenna's boots made sloshing sounds as she walked, slowly at first, then her pace increasing as her feet made the destination decision for her. She cut down a side street, then another, avoiding the main downtown area.

An expanse of green opened up before her, dotted with piles here and there of leftover snow. Most of the Winterfest decorations had been removed from the park, leaving it in its natural state, a little barer because of winter, but still a quiet, peaceful haven.

She'd come here hundreds of times when she'd been a little girl, and even into her teen years. Maybe it was because the open space reminded her so much of the farm she'd lived on when she'd been younger, or maybe it was just that the Riverbend park, with its lush green trees and winding paths, offered a quiet refuge from the hundreds of changes in one little girl's life.

The paths had been plowed, which made walking along the nearly clean pavement much easier. Jenna took her time, not really looking at her surroundings, but breathing them in, letting the crisp air fill her lungs.

But it wasn't enough. She walked farther, and still the knot of tension that had come with her from New York nagged at her neck. She kept heading down the paths, as if distance would change everything.

This place is home for you, Jenna. It always was, Earl had said. Was he right? Had all these past few months of feeling misdirected, and bringing that misdirection to work, mean she was fighting, as Aunt Mabel told her, against what her subconscious really wanted?

Did a part of her want to be back here?

And call Riverbend home?

The thought chafed at her, like a new scab on an old wound. She danced around it in her mind, not sure if it was right, or just the cold muddling her thoughts.

The trees surrounded her like quiet sentries. Far in the distance, she heard the happy laughter of skaters on the pond, the crackle of melting snow falling to the ground, the titters of squirrels enjoying the warmer weather.

She increased her pace, letting the cold air and the long cement paths take her mind off the past few days. She walked fast, intent only on the road ahead, the next curve, the tree at the end where the road turned toward the playground.

"Jenna!"

The shout caught her by surprise and she stumbled, her foot hitting a patch of ice. Just as she was about to meet the pavement, a strong pair of arms scooped her up and righted her again. Stockton.

"Thanks." She shot him a smile.

"Just doing my gentlemanly duty, ma'am." He swept forward into a quick bow, which made her laugh. The tense knot in her neck eased, and a lightness filled her chest.

"Stockton Grisham, always to the rescue."

"I've been saving you ever since second grade," Stockton said, "when you fell on the playground—"

"And you carried me all the way to the nurse's office." She smiled at the memory, then dug her hands into her coat pockets, and started walking again. Stockton kept pace beside her, and for a second, it felt like old times, when they used to walk to and from school together. In the days when she could confide anything to him, and know that he would support, not judge.

"So tomorrow you go back to New York," he said. "Back to business as usual."

"I hope it's not business as usual. That's the last thing I need." She saw his quizzical glance. "In the last few months, I've been…off my game, I guess you'd say. I've started forgetting appointments, and doing stupid things like scheduling DJs and caterers for the wrong dates."

"Maybe you're just burned out."

"Maybe." The thought of going back to her apartment, back to the city, didn't fill her with the same anticipation as always. She glanced around the park, at the trees dusted with white, the rolling hills that would be green in the spring, and the circular beds that would bloom with flowers in a few months. It was quiet and peaceful, the kind of environment where someone could get lost in their thoughts. Where she lived was so busy, with the constant hum of traffic and construction. Still, New York was where her business was, where her things were…and where she belonged. Wasn't it? "I've got a lot waiting for me back there."

"You have a lot here, too."

She stopped walking and looked at him. "Like what, Stockton? You? We keep dancing around this, and neither one of us is really saying anything."

"What is it that I'm supposed to say?" He let out a gust of frustration and his gaze went past her, to the bare trees, their tall skinny trunks vulnerable and stark against the white snowy backdrop. "What are you expecting out of these few days? Because from what I see, all you want to do is get out of town again."

"And all you want to do is escape with your heart intact, like in the old days," she said.

"That's not true."

"It isn't?" In that moment, the years of distance between them was erased, and the old hurt roared to the surface. "Eight years ago, you let me go. Watched me get on that plane and let me leave. Because you were too scared to take a risk, and go with me. To stay in one place with one person."

"And what, watch you bury yourself in your work? Maybe you don't remember, Jenna, but you had only one setting in your mind. Forward."

"There's nothing wrong with ambition. You're ambitious, too. It's what has made your restaurant a success. And yet you criticize me for having the same goals?"

"Yeah, when it's at the expense of relationships with people who care about you."

His words were cold, sharp. But she noticed one thing lacking in them. The word *I*. He hadn't said relationships with him, or that he cared about her. He'd kept it vague, unconnected. "I could say the same for you," she said.

"Is that what you think I'm doing? Because last I checked, I was the one who was staying here in town and you were the one getting on the first plane out of here."

She sighed. "You know, you keep telling me I should change my life. What about you? You spend virtually all your waking hours in this restaurant, so you don't have to risk having a real, in-depth relationship. You're as much of a wanderer today as you were before. Taking the easy way out instead of sticking around."

"Is that what you think, Jenna? That I took the easy way out?"

She arched a brow. "Didn't you? With us?"

"You're wrong. Watching you go to New York was the hard way." He let out a breath that formed a soft cloud around his lips. "The easy route would have been to follow you and pretend we could make it work. Done what everyone expected me to do." He paused a beat. "And marry you."

The last two words hung in the air for a long, long time. "Well, at least you avoided that mistake," Jenna said after a moment.

"Yeah." The word was short, curt and devoid of any inflection that could tell Jenna if Stockton was regretful or grateful. "I didn't go to New York, Jenna, because I wanted…" He shook his head. "I wanted more."

"What more?"

"A way to fill the emptiness," he said after a moment, and an alarm sounded in Jenna's head. Was that what she'd been feeling in these past few months? An emptiness that she needed to fill in a new way?

"I traveled for a while," Stockton went on, "exploring new cuisines, new customs. All the while, I was thinking it wasn't the place that had felt wrong, it was…" He shrugged. "Me. In the end, the only place I wanted to serve a meal was right here, in my hometown. Riverbend is my home, and always has been. I just didn't know it until I left. So I came home. And stayed."

Stockton had a physical address that wasn't changing, but in all these days together, she still hadn't heard what she needed to hear from him—that his emotional address was locked, too. That he was ready to settle down with one person and take a risk on love. That had always been the problem between them—she was looking for more from him than he was willing to give. In the end, nothing had changed between them. Nothing at all.

She drew her coat tighter, even though the outdoor temperature hadn't changed. The chill in the air was entirely between her and Stockton. "Eunice's party is tomorrow," she said, avoiding the conversational powderkeg that

Stockton seemed determined to light. "Are you all set with the menu?"

Disappointment dropped a shadow over his face. "I guess that's it then. There's really nothing else for us to discuss." He gave her one quick, short nod. "I'll see you tomorrow."

And then he was gone, leaving her alone in a park that had once seemed peaceful and wonderful had become cold and empty.

CHAPTER TWELVE

WHEN GRACE, THE HOSTESS, had come to Stockton and said there was a woman waiting to see him, his first thought was Jenna. He smoothed his shirt, ran a hand through his hair and pushed through the kitchen's doors, a smile ready on his face.

But Livia, not Jenna, stood by the hostess station, an envelope in her hands and a sympathetic look in her eyes. "I came by to give you the balance for the catering for Eunice's party." She held up the envelope.

"Oh." Stockton took it, then stuffed it into his back pocket. "Thanks."

"For what it's worth, I told her that avoiding a problem didn't make it go away. Jenna's pretty good at that, you know. Avoiding." Livia started to walk off, then turned back. "And hey, one thing about Jenna that you should know—she's a tough cookie, but inside, she's a bunch of crumbs."

"She's made it clear that she's going back to New York, Livia."

"If you ask me, she keeps saying that because she's waiting for someone to give her a reason to stay."

"You're leaving? Now?" Livia's eyes widened. Behind her, the staff of the banquet hall was busy ironing the tablecloths and setting out silverware. Across the room, Edward was ostensibly watching his staff, but more, Jenna suspected, waiting for Livia to be free.

"I'll be back before you know it. I have an errand to run. It won't take long, I promise." Jenna handed the event folder over to Livia. In it was the detailed plan for Eunice's party, not that Livia, who was a stickler for detail, would have forgotten any of the necessary components. "We've got everything pretty much all set up. The florist should be here in the next half hour, and I'll be back in time to set up the arrangements." Then she grabbed her purse, headed out the door and into the winter sunshine. She drove to Aunt Mabel's house, ran upstairs and grabbed her suitcase. It took a couple of minutes to gather what she wanted, put the items into another bag, then head back out to her rental car.

A few minutes later, she pulled up in front of the church. The vestry was empty when she stepped inside, and the quiet of the ornate room enveloped her like a blanket. It seemed everywhere she went in Riverbend, she found peace and quiet.

Which came with the dual-edged sword of space to think. She'd spent the past two days doing nothing but thinking, it seemed. She'd done a mental dance around the answers she sought, and every time, come back to this. To the people and place that had reminded her of what was important.

Jenna strode down the carpeted aisle of the St. Francis church, then detoured through a pew to reach the side door. The community room at the bottom of the stairs was empty, tables and chairs neatly stacked against the wall, the floor gleaming and freshly mopped. Jenna followed the sound of voices into a small room with a television and a trio of sofas.

"Jenna!" The priest greeted her when she stepped into the room, striding forward with an outstretched hand. "So nice to see you again."

"Same to you." She smiled.

"You just missed Stockton."

"Oh." The sound of his name hit her hard, but she forced herself to keep that smile on her face. A few more hours and she'd be gone, far from Stockton.

Since yesterday, Jenna had made sure to avoid him. She'd had Livia deliver the final payment for the catering, and begged off when Aunt Mabel invited her to Rustica for dinner last night. She'd pled a headache, and tried not to cry when Aunt Mabel brought her back a takeout order of lasagna with a side of béchamel sauce.

Why drag out the inevitable? She was leaving, and he was staying.

"If you stay around a while," Father Michael said, "you can get a listen of the band that's setting up." He gestured toward the main hall, where several men were assembling musical equipment. Jenna recognized two of them from the day she'd been here serving breakfast.

"Band? What for?"

"We're going to have a fundraiser in the spring. To raise money for the shelter." Father Michael tapped her arm. "I heard you handled one of those before."

"I did. It raised four hundred thousand dollars for breast cancer research."

Father Michael let out a low whistle. "That's amazing."

She nodded. "It was one of the most rewarding moments of my career."

"Perhaps you should consider giving us a hand, then," Father Michael said. "Since you are the pro at this."

She shook her head. "I'm sorry, but I'm leaving tonight. I have to get back to New York."

"Of course. I understand." Father Michael looked as if he wanted to say more, but one of the band members called him over to the stage.

As he walked away, Jenna's mind began rolling down the road the priest had presented. She thought of how she'd handle such a fundraiser. How she'd organize the promotion, create a theme that would get people talking, and do it all with a budget that gave maximum dollars to the shelter.

She glanced to her right and saw Tammy in the kitchen, working on a potato salad. She remembered the bundle in her arms, and headed into the gleaming galley-style space. "Hey, Tammy."

"Oh, hi, Jenna. What are you doing here?"

"I brought these for you." She held up two of her business suits. When she'd pulled them out of her suitcase, she'd been sure the dark blue one would be the best for Tammy's complexion, and now, holding it up and near Tammy's peach skin, she saw she was right. "I think this color would look great on you."

Tammy beamed, and the joy in her features sent warmth spreading through Jenna. She thought of her overstuffed closet in her apartment, brimming with clothes she'd stopped wearing or didn't need, and realized she could make a small, very small difference, here in Riverbend. How many suits did one woman need anyway?

It wouldn't be enough to repay those people who had made a difference in her life, but it would be a start. And for the first time since she arrived in Riverbend, Jenna felt a sense of connection to the town. The knot of tension in her neck that had seemed a constant companion slowly loosened.

"Oh, my goodness. Thank you so much," Tammy said,

running a gentle hand over the soft wool fabric. "These are wonderful. I really appreciate it."

Jenna glanced out to the front room again, where the men had gathered with the priest, presumably to discuss the upcoming fundraising event. Once again, a list of ideas danced in Jenna's mind. She could feel the familiar buzz of anticipation in her gut, the same feeling that she'd once had when she'd opened her business.

Was that what had caused her to lose her touch? Was that why she couldn't seem to get back on track? Because all the engagement parties and birthday parties and corporate dinners had seemed so...empty?

Fundraising. Making a difference. The knot of tension disappeared completely as the idea formed in Jenna's mind. She turned back to Tammy. "Listen, I know you're interviewing for another job, but I was wondering if you'd like to work with me on a project here."

"Work with you? On what?"

"Father Michael wants to hold a fundraiser for the shelter. I'd offer to organize it, but since I live in New York, I'll need a local contact to handle a lot of the details." She thought of the gregarious, organized woman she'd known in high school. What better person could she call on for help? "I think you'd be great at that."

"Really?" Tammy's eyes widened, first with shock, then with hope. "You think so?"

Jenna nodded. "I do."

Tammy stepped forward and enveloped Jenna in a tight, earnest hug. "Thank you. Thank you so much. You've changed more than just my outfit today, Jenna."

As Jenna returned Tammy's embrace, she thought about the circle of life. Twenty-plus years ago, her family had been the one in need. In this very basement, people had filled that need, receiving gratitude in return. She saw now why people helped others—the return on investment was far greater than the work involved. This, she realized, was exactly what she had been searching for.

The only problem was that she was returning to New York, to the same world that had drained her. And leaving all this behind.

The room was ready. After returning from dropping off her suits at the church, Jenna had spent the rest of the day at the banquet hall with Livia, putting the finishing touches on the tables, adding the rest of the photos, and setting up the flowers. Livia had left to go back to Aunt Mabel's and change, while Jenna slipped into the hall's ladies' room and switched from jeans and a T-shirt to a little black dress with heels that she'd bought yesterday.

She checked her reflection, smoothed her hair and touched up her makeup. She was ready, too. She stepped out of the ladies' room and took in the ballroom one more time. Everything was in its place, as it should be. A multi-tiered cake in yellow and pink—Eunice's favorite colors—sat against one wall, while two long tables lined with photographs sat against the other. The centerpieces representing each decade anchored the tables and provided a visual history of the past hundred years. Helium-filled pink and yellow balloons stood in massive bouquets throughout the room while a giant banner congratulating Eunice on her hundredth birthday dominated the wall behind the head table.

For a second, she thought of the party she'd helped plan at Stockton's restaurant. New Year's Eve, supposed to be the night of new beginnings, new resolutions. And all she'd done that night was complicate her life by kissing him.

And worse, falling for him again.

In the past two weeks, Stockton Grisham, with his sexy

smile and patient approach to everything, had done the one thing Jenna swore he'd never do again—infiltrated her heart. She didn't know when, but somewhere between the ice skating and the kiss on the dance floor, he'd reawakened feelings she'd thought no longer existed.

But it was no fun to travel a relationship road by herself. She might be ready to settle down, but she hadn't seen one sign that Stockton was any more ready now than he had been eight years ago.

She checked her watch. In an hour, Eunice's birthday party would begin. And in five hours, she would be gone, on her way to the airport with Livia. Returning to her city life, and leaving this small town behind for good. For Jenna, it wasn't soon enough.

The side door opened, spilling bright light into the hall. A silhouette of a man filled the doorway and Jenna's heart tripped.

Stockton.

It didn't matter how often her brain told her that they were over, the rest of her didn't seem to listen. And now, with her departure so near, an ache began to build in her chest. Telling Jenna Pearson that leaving Riverbend was going to be harder than she'd thought.

"I've got the food," Stockton said. "I'll need to set up in the kitchen. Shouldn't take very long."

Nothing personal in his statement. All business.

Exactly the way she wanted it. After all, hadn't she made it clear to him that she was leaving? That after today, they would go back to where they had been—living in separate states, no longer together. Still, a persistent feeling of disappointment hung heavy in her stomach. She pushed it away. *Get through this party, and everything will be okay.*

Stockton hefted a large insulated container into his arms, then entered the hall. Jenna hurried over to the doors leading to the kitchen, holding them open for him to pass through. It wasn't until he reached her, and the gap between them closed from feet to inches that she realized her mistake. Holding the doors put her almost skin to skin with him. She caught the woodsy notes of his cologne, noticed the way his dark hair curled a little along the edge of his neck, the warmth emanating from his body. Everything inside her ignored common sense, and sent a hot surge of desire through her veins.

"Thanks," Stockton said, as if he'd been completely unaffected.

"No problem." Once he was in the kitchen, she stepped away, letting the door shut on her hormones.

But not her emotions.

Hurt bubbled over inside her, and as much as she tried to ignore it, told herself she was over him, that the kisses they had shared had been nothing more than a crazy indulgence in old feelings, still the pain of his coldness stuck. That once again, he was letting her leave.

He carried in a half-dozen containers, all without much more than exchanging a few pleasantries with her. *Hasn't this weather been nice? How long do you think the higher temperatures will last? Surely, Eunice will love the food...*

Things like that, all impersonal. Nothing about their conversations over the last few days, nothing about the kisses they had exchanged. It was as if she was dealing with an ordinary vendor, not a man she had a personal, complicated history with. Not a man she was about to say goodbye to for the second time in her life, in just a few hours.

After the last container was loaded into the kitchen, Stockton called out to Jenna. "Would you mind giving me a hand for a second? I've got some of the waitstaff coming over but I hate to waste even a second when it comes to hot food."

She glanced around the room one more time, ensuring the flowers were in place, the centerpieces laid out according to her plan, the linens neat and pressed. Livia would be arriving any minute to give the room a second set of eyes. Every time she planned a party, Jenna felt as if she couldn't go over the details enough. She'd fret and stew, and pace and straighten—

She'd be better off in the kitchen, keeping busy, so she wouldn't get too obsessive over a simple birthday party.

"I have a few minutes," she said, then entered the kitchen and donned an apron. Surely she could spend these few minutes with Stockton and stay immune to his charm.

"A little bit of déjà vu, isn't it?" Stockton said, as he slipped on an apron emblazoned with Rustica's name and logo. "You and me, working together. Just like two weeks ago, when you helped in the restaurant."

"And burned a sauce, if you remember right. I'm not exactly sous chef material." She started pouring hot water into the chafing dish bases, so they would keep the food warm and moist once the burners underneath were lit. "You know, we worked together in a kitchen once before."

Stockton paused in the middle of pouring rolls into a huge glass bowl. "We did? When?"

"Home ec. Tenth grade. We were kitchen partners for cooking class."

He laughed, and the light sound eased the worries in Jenna's chest. Stockton had always been able to do that with her—make her forget her troubles and find something sweet to celebrate about her day. His lighthearted approach to things had been the perfect antidote to a girl who wanted to forget the heavy past that dogged her. "I forgot about that. Probably because it was such a disaster."

She wagged a finger at him. "*You* burned the cookies."

"I was distracted." He reached for another bag of rolls.

"That wasn't it at all. You weren't much of a baker, admit it."

He crossed to her, and for a second, she thought he was going to kiss her again. Instead, he reached past her for a container of butter. Disappointment fell like a stone in her stomach. God, she was a mess. Didn't know what she wanted from one minute to the next. "I wasn't much of a baker. And I was distracted." He paused a second, his gaze locking on hers. "I still am."

Jenna swallowed hard. "By what?"

"By you." Then he backed away, and laid the butter beside the rolls.

Her laughter shook a little. She went back to filling the pitcher with hot water and transferring it to the chafing dishes. "It looks like we'll have close to two hundred people here tonight. A lot of people from town are coming, and Eunice's cousin from Pennsylvania is—"

"Are we going to talk about it or not?"

"Talk about what?"

"About you leaving. Every time I bring it up, you change the subject."

The last of the dishes had been filled. Jenna put the pitcher into the sink, then turned around and faced Stockton. She crossed her arms over her chest, as if that was any kind of barrier between them. "I'm better off in New York, Stockton."

"Are you?"

She threw up her hands. "What's that supposed to mean?"

"Are you happy? With your life? Your job?"

"Of course I am." But just as it had with Stockton, Jenna could hear the answer coming too fast, too pat.

He shook his head and studied her. "I've known you almost all your life, and I'm telling you, you aren't happy. You can go back to New York, go back to your business, and tell yourself this is exactly what you wanted, but I think you're going to find the same thing I did."

"What's that?"

"That there's a hole in your life that no amount of distance can fill."

It was as if he'd read her mind, and still, she resisted. She kept thinking how he was just letting her go. It was eight years ago, all over again, and Jenna could barely stand to watch the inevitable conclusion unfold. "There is no hole, Stockton. And if I seem off or whatever you think, it's stress, nothing more." She waved toward the room set up for the party. "Out in that room, that's my job—" and then she thumbed in an easterly direction "—and there's my life, several states away."

He shrugged. "Okay, if that's the way you want it." He closed the emptied insulated containers, and carried them out the door and back to his truck.

"It is," she said, but Stockton was no longer in the room, and the only person she was telling was herself.

CHAPTER THIRTEEN

STOCKTON HOVERED NEAR the buffet table, greeting the people he knew and refilling the dishes as needed. He could have hidden in the kitchen, but some masochistic urge kept him out here, with Jenna only feet away. The guests talked among themselves, filling in the silence because the band was late. Jenna had been on the phone, trying to reach them, her face flushed with frustration.

"Stockton! Come on over here, young man." Betsy waved at him from the head table.

He crossed to Betsy, Earl, Jenna's aunt Mabel, and Eunice, and several other members of Eunice's family that he didn't recognize. "Yes, ma'am?"

"Thank you for making my birthday meal," Eunice said. "You know how I love those toasted raviolis."

"I do indeed." He cupped a hand around his mouth. "And I made sure to put extras aside for you to take home."

Eunice giggled like a girl. "Thank you, Stockton."

"Anything for you, Mrs. Dresden." He pressed a kiss to her L'Air du Temps scented cheek and wished her a happy birthday.

"Enough about the meal," Betsy said. "When are you going to do something about our Jenna?"

"Excuse me?"

"You aren't seriously going to let her go back to New York, are you?"

"I don't think I get a vote."

"Of course you do," Aunt Mabel cut in. "If you ask me, yours is the only vote that matters."

"There's Jenna's."

Aunt Mabel waved a hand. "That girl doesn't know what's good for her when it's standing ten feet away. Come to think of it, neither do you."

He chuckled. "Aunt Mabel, I most certainly know what's good for me."

She shooed at him. "Then go get it, and quit standing around this table, moping like a puppy that's lost his tennis ball."

Jenna's aunt couldn't have been more obvious if she'd hung up a sign ordering Stockton to propose to her niece. "Aunt Mabel, you are a terrible matchmaker."

"I don't know about that," Earl cut in. "She told me I should call on Miss Betsy here, that it'd be the best thing I ever did. And what do you know? Mabel was right."

"Oh, Earl," Betsy said, feigning annoyance, but her cheeks colored with pleasure.

Aunt Mabel frowned at Stockton. "I'm too old to have my remaining family scattered to the four corners of the world."

"New York is hardly the other side of the universe."

"It is to me, and it will be to you if you don't get smart, young man." Aunt Mabel pushed a box across the table to him. "Inside that box is Jenna's grandmother's engagement ring. Her father put it on her mother's finger, and her mother promised her that when she was ready to get married, it would be hers. I've kept it all these years, waiting for the right man to come along for my Jenna."

"Aunt Mabel—"

"You keep it, Stockton. Even if I was mad as heck at you for letting her get away the first time, I've always known you were the right man for her. Now it's just time you and Jenna realized that."

Stockton put the ring in his pocket. Later, he'd return it to Aunt Mabel. For now, it seemed easier just to keep it and appease everyone. But as he walked away and felt the heft of the ring box, he wondered if maybe this was a case of his elders knowing better than he did.

Jenna watched the exchange between her aunt and Stockton, but didn't hear what they'd said. She thought she saw her aunt give something to Stockton, but what it was, she didn't know. Whatever that had been about, it was all classic Aunt Mabel—interfering for the sweetest of reasons, and over the objections of the niece she had raised.

Right now, Jenna had more important things to worry about, like MIA musicians. She dialed her phone again, and once again, there was no answer.

Livia crossed to Jenna's side, and handed her a revised schedule for the day. "Things seem to be going pretty well."

"Except for the band not showing up. Where are they? Do you think they got lost?"

"I faxed the directions myself," Livia said. "And it's not like this town is so huge you can't find your way around."

Jenna laid a hand on her friend's shoulder. "I don't think I ever thanked you enough for flying down here and helping me with this party."

"I didn't do much. I was more moral support than anything else."

Jenna laughed. Gratitude for friends like Livia washed over her. "Well, either way, you're getting a paycheck at the end of this. And hopefully, the success of this party will turn into more when we get back to New York."

Livia toed at the floor, her bell-shaped skirt making a soft swish. "About New York…" She glanced up at Jenna and grimaced. "I don't think I'm going back tonight."

"Do you want to take a later flight? I can change our reservation."

"I meant I don't think I'm going back…ever." Livia's gaze swept over the room and settled on one person. A smile curved up her face as her gaze lingered on Edward Graham's tall, lean frame. "Seems I've been offered a job."

"A job? Where?"

"Here." The smile widened. "Edward said he needs someone to run the Riverbend Banquet Hall for him. And…" she let out a deep breath "…he's asked me to do it."

Edward caught Livia looking at him, and he tossed her a smile back. Livia practically hummed with joy.

A whisper of envy ran through Jenna. "That's wonderful, Livia. Though I think he has an ulterior motive for offering you the job."

"And I have an ulterior motive for accepting." Livia laughed, then sobered. "I'm sorry, Jenna. I really love working with you, but this town kind of grew on me in the last few days and I think this will be a great opportunity for me."

"I think it will, too," Jenna said, then drew Livia into a hug.

"You're going to do great when you get back home. I know you will."

Home. The word didn't seem to hold the same meaning it once did. Jenna told herself it was only because she'd been away from her apartment for so many days. That once she stepped back into the busy city, everything would be fine.

Wouldn't it?

She looked around the banquet hall, filled to brimming with a lifetime's worth of friends in Eunice's life. It took living in the same place, year after year, to build up this kind of close circle. In her neighborhood in New York, there were people who had known each other for decades, and surely, some of the same kind of relationships as Eunice had here.

The difference? Eunice had lived in Riverbend all her life. She was the quintessential small-town girl. As Jenna watched Eunice laugh and chat with person after person, she realized their memories wrapped around Eunice like a blanket. A part of Jenna, a part she had always shushed, craved that blanket for herself. Her mind went back to Tammy, to Father Michael, to the people she had seen working together for the common good, and wondered if maybe she was looking in the wrong place.

Her cell phone rang, jarring her out of her reverie. In a halting, apologetic voice, the drummer of the missing band confirmed Jenna's worst nightmare. She sighed and hung up the phone, then turned to Livia. "The band isn't going to make it." God, this was just like all the mistakes she'd made in New York. Was she ever going to get out of this rut?

"I thought you had them booked."

"They were, but apparently the band double-booked. The band leader didn't tell the guitarist that they had other plans already, and the guitarist went ahead and made an agreement with someone else. Right now, they're in Indianapolis, playing at someone's wedding."

"Oh, no. That stinks."

Jenna paced in a circle. "I can't believe I did this again.

I double-checked with them, but I should have triple-checked. Quadruple-checked."

"This one's not your fault. They double-booked, not you."

Jenna waved toward the head table, where Eunice sat with her closest friends and family members, waiting for the music to start and her birthday party to get fully underway. "Tell that to Betsy. She's just been waiting for me to screw up. She told me this was the most important day of Eunice's life and I had to get it right."

"But you did. Everything is arranged as it should be, and it all looks great."

"Except it's a bit quiet in here." Jenna paced again, tapping her phone against her chin. "I need to fix this. Now."

"In a town this size, where are you going to find a band on such short notice?"

Jenna flipped out her phone, and dialed another number. "I have an idea."

Ten minutes later, Betsy was marching across the room, her face a mask of anger. "Why is there no music?"

"I'm taking care of it. Give me fifteen minutes."

Betsy let out a frustrated gust. "I hired you to provide a perfect party for my sister's birthday. And now..." She threw up her hands.

"It will be perfect, I promise."

"Your aunt said you were the best. If you ask me, this is far from best."

"Now, Miss Betsy, not all of us can meet your high expectations." Stockton's voice was quiet, cajoling. "Everyone in Riverbend knows if they want someone who goes above and beyond, they need to stay at Betsy's Bed and Breakfast."

Her chin jutted up. "Of course. I run my business very efficiently."

Jenna glanced at Stockton and wondered where he was going with this. "That you do," Jenna agreed.

"And yet, I'm sure even you have had days when things didn't go as planned," Stockton went on. "Guests who arrived unexpectedly or a dinner that didn't turn out quite as you expected."

"Or the plumbing breaking at the worst possible time," Betsy said with a frown at the memory. "Right in the middle of a family reunion, too. Goodness, what a stink. Literally."

"Exactly," Jenna chimed in, with a grateful smile for Stockton. "And I'm sure all you wanted your guests to do was relax, enjoy themselves and give you a minute to rectify the situation. Like call another band to come in and replace the one that couldn't make it."

It took a moment, but the anger washed from Betsy's features, replaced by understanding. She nodded. "I'll go back to the table. Get Eunice to share her top five memories with the guests. That should be enough time until the music arrives."

"Thank you," Jenna said. "That's all I need."

Betsy patted Jenna's arm, and in her eyes, she read something more than agreement. She saw acceptance, warmth. "We all have little glitches," Betsy said.

"We do. And in the end, I think it will all work out fine."

Betsy considered Jenna again for a long time, then nodded and smiled. "I have no doubt it will. No doubt at all."

Twenty minutes later, the band was on the stage and launching into a bluesy-jazz mix of oldies but goodies. Across the room, Jenna saw Eunice nodding with the music, clearly pleased with the choices. The guests chatted and laughed, and she overheard several comments about the excellence of the food, the cool factor of the decorations, and the memories seeing Eunice's photographs had evoked.

The party was a success. She'd done it—and she'd done it well. It was going to take some hard work, but she could bring her business back from the brink of disaster. In her pocket, she patted her plane ticket, and told herself she'd be back on top in no time.

As she made her way through the room, checking and double-checking that the food was still hot, the photographs still in the right order and the guests happy and fed, an odd sense that she was missing something filled Jenna. At first, she thought she'd overlooked something for the party. Forgotten a place setting or the guest book or some other detail.

No, that wasn't it. Everything was where it should be. Still, she couldn't shake the feeling.

Father Michael walked over to Jenna, and shook her hand. "Thank you," she said. "You really pulled off a miracle for me at the last minute."

He waved off her gratitude. "I didn't do anything but drive the van that got the band here. You did something much bigger."

"What's that?"

"You gave them a second chance." He waved toward the band. "And that's something that can't be bought. You did it for Tammy, too. Goodness, Jenna, you're making changes all over this town. People will miss you when you leave, that's for sure."

"Oh, I don't know about that."

Father Michael's gaze swept the room, then came back to Jenna's face. "I think you need to have a closer look at all the friendly faces here. This is your home, Jenna. It always was." Then he walked off toward the band.

Her home. Hadn't Earl said pretty much the same thing? For so long, she'd resisted that thought, sure that she could never feel truly at home in a town where the whispers about her parents were a constant hum around her. She'd been too busy listening to that hum to appreciate the rest of the town. To realize it offered a connection, one she had foolishly left behind.

And then, she knew. What she had been looking for all along wasn't success, or a great party, but this—

This people connection that showed she had made a difference. She'd handled dozens and dozens of parties, but after all the flowers were dead and the decorations taken down, what had she been left with? A sense that she'd thrown a great party, sure, but there'd always been that little sense of *is this it?*

She brushed off the questions. She didn't have time to deal with them now—she needed to keep her focus until Eunice's party ended. She headed over to the buffet line, and a moment later, Stockton joined her. "Thank you for what you did with Betsy."

"No problem. You know her as well as I do. She can have a temper, but she can also be fair and understanding."

Jenna nodded her agreement. She gestured toward the head table, where the group with Eunice was chatting, laughing and eating their second helping of Rustica's entrées. "So what was that all about with my aunt and Betsy?"

"The food." He grinned. "And you."

Jenna groaned. "Do I want to ask?"

He chuckled. "No, you really don't."

Undoubtedly, her aunt was playing matchmaker, one of the roles she liked best. Jenna decided to stay far, far away from that topic. Stockton had dropped the subject of her staying in Riverbend, and seemed fine with the fact that she was leaving for good in a few hours.

She tried not to let the disappointment swell in her chest, but it did all the same.

With all the guests served, Stockton began cleaning up the buffet while the waitstaff carried in the empty plates and dirty silverware. Stockton hefted the massive, and nearly empty, bowl of salad into his arms and headed for the kitchen. Jenna grabbed the container of rolls and followed after him.

She found him in the kitchen, busy scraping the leftovers into a small container, then loading the dirty bowl into the sink. Silence extended between them, while outside the double doors the room's chatter continued at a happy hum, set to the beat of the band's soft rock tunes.

She watched him work, watched the movements of his lean frame, the way his jaw set in concentration. She knew Stockton better than she knew anyone else. Could have drawn his features in her sleep. And she had loved him nearly all that time.

How was she going to leave this town? Leave him again? It had been so hard for her to get on the plane to New York the first time. She'd told herself at the time that she was making the right decision, the one that was best for both of them. Eight years ago, it had felt right.

But now… Now it hurt.

The kitchen doors swung open and Livia strode into the small space. "Hey, sorry to interrupt, but it's time to sing happy birthday to Eunice and let her blow out the candles."

"Great," Jenna said, although she was feeling far from festive. Birthday cake meant the end of the party was nearly here, and she'd be that much closer to putting Riverbend and Stockton far behind her.

Jenna left the kitchen, then signaled to the band. As they launched into "Happy Birthday," Jenna and Livia wheeled the cake in front of the head table. Jenna lit the three numeral-shaped candles spelling out the number one hundred—much better than the overwhelming option of a full hundred candles—while Eunice came around to stand before her cake. "It's beautiful," she said. "Goodness gracious. I can't believe I'm a hundred years old. I still feel ninety." She laughed.

Someone called "speech, speech" from across the room. Another voice asked, "What's your advice for living to be one hundred?"

Eunice thought a second, her hands clasped at her waist. "Find what truly makes you happy, and living to an old age will be easy."

The ballroom erupted in applause, the band launched into "Happy Birthday" and the crowd began to sing to Eunice. She leaned forward, paused, as if she was making a wish, then she blew out all three candles. There was another, more enthusiastic round of applause, then Jenna and Livia took the cake back to the kitchen to cut it into serving pieces.

"I can do this with Jenna," Stockton said to Livia. "You go keep Edward company."

"I'm not turning that offer down," Livia said. She thanked Stockton, then left the kitchen, a wide smile of anticipation on her face. Jenna suspected it'd be a long time before that smile disappeared, given the way things were going between Livia and the owner of the banquet hall.

"Looks like Eunice's party was a success," Stockton said to Jenna as he dipped a long cake knife into hot water and began slicing through the dessert. With deft movements, he cut off squares and loaded them onto plates that the waitstaff then put onto trays. As he did, Jenna added dessert forks to each serving. The waitstaff moved in and out of the kitchen, delivering the cake to the guests before returning for more.

"Things did go very well, even with that little glitch with the band," Jenna said. "I'm pleased, not just for my company, but for Eunice. And for you. This should help spread the word that Rustica is one of the best restaurants in Indiana."

Stockton sliced the last piece, then put the knife down. "You know, I didn't take on this job because it would help my business, Jenna." He considered his words for a second. "Maybe I did at first, but then it became something more."

Jenna propped a fork onto the small plate, set it on the tray, then faced Stockton. There was nothing left to do, not really, except finally deal with what they had been dancing around for days. "What do you mean?"

"I did this because I wanted answers." He leaned back against the stainless steel countertop. He wore his white chef jacket and dress pants, but to Jenna, he had never looked more handsome. She wanted to reach out and touch him, to kiss him just one more time before she left.

She stayed where she was. Trying to be wise, not rash.

"Answers about us," he said.

"Us?" Her heart beat faster, and her breath caught in her throat.

"You asked me why I didn't come after you when you went to New York." His blue gaze met hers, so direct she was sure he could see inside her.

She shrugged, as if the topic didn't send a sword through her heart. As if bringing up those awful days didn't still hurt like hell. "I just assumed if you wanted to be with me, you would have come after me. You didn't, so..." A long breath escaped her. "So that was it."

He pushed off from the countertop and closed the gap between them. Her pulse began to race, and as she looked over his face, her mind repeated one phrase over and over again.

This is the last time you're going to see him.

Because even if she returned to Riverbend after this, to visit with her aunt, or to see Livia, she knew, deep in her heart, that she would not be with Stockton again. They had reached some kind of pivotal moment in their relationship, a door that had been opened by the catering job, and she was about to let that door shut.

Once it did, she sensed whatever feelings might have remained between them would die. It would be over. For good.

"I always wondered why you left so abruptly."

"It was the end of the summer. I had a job offer at a party planning company, and there was an opening at the college there for the hospitality program—"

"Which meant you'd planned this, at least a little."

She bit her lip. "I just couldn't find the right time to tell you."

"Was it really that?" he asked quietly. "Or did you drop that bombshell and hop on the next plane so you could leave me before I left you?"

"I..." Her protest died on her lips. She thought of those last few months when they'd been dating. Stockton had talked about traveling the world, then coming back to Riverbend. All she heard, though, was "leaving town." She was so sure—so, so sure—that he'd never return. That he'd find someone else in another city.

"People are going to leave you, people are going to disappoint you. So why not force that process along a little bit?"

"I didn't…" She sighed and shook her head as tears worked their way to the surface. She thought of all the people who had left her, or let her down. Her parents dying, her world turning upside-down. Had she done that to Stockton, too? Been so ready for someone else to leave her that she did it to them first? "Okay, maybe I did. But how can you blame me for a little self-preservation? By the time we graduated high school, I realized all your talk about traveling the world was so you could get away from the one thing you've always avoided like the plague. Commitment."

"My schedule is insane, Jenna. Even if I wanted to have a family—"

"If you want something bad enough, you get it, Stockton. You did it with your restaurant. You bucked all the odds, silenced the naysayers. You did it. But when it comes to your personal life…you don't take that same risk. And you know why?" She didn't wait for an answer. "Because you're guarding something, too. That's the part you've given to your restaurant instead of to other people." Her hand flattened against the left side of his chest. "The one thing I could never have, no matter how hard I tried. Your heart."

She stepped away and headed for the swinging door of the kitchen. "That's why I'm going back to New York, Stockton. Because I know better than to wait around for something I'm never going to have."

CHAPTER FOURTEEN

NIGHT HAD FALLEN, bathing Riverbend in a nearly silent darkness. Like most small towns, everything buttoned down once the sun went down. Most of the shops were closed, the traffic disappeared and even the neighbor's dogs seemed to quiet their barks. Jenna stood in the bedroom she had lived in since she was seven years old and added the last of her sweaters to her suitcase. "I'm all packed."

Aunt Mabel sighed. "I wish you wouldn't go."

Jenna turned and drew her aunt into a tight hug. "I'll be back soon, I promise."

"I'm going to hold you to that," Aunt Mabel said. "And please, don't let so much time go by next time."

Jenna laughed, then went back to her suitcase while Aunt Mabel took a seat on the bed. "You could always come to New York and visit me, Aunt Mabel."

"I could. And while I was there, I could stock up on that coffee you're always sending me." Aunt Mabel smoothed a hand over the quilt at the end of Jenna's bed. "Or...you could call Percival Mullins."

Jenna glanced around the room, but didn't see anything she'd left behind. The bathroom, had she gotten everything in there? Either way, if she forgot anything, her aunt would send it to her. Still, the persistent feeling that she was leaving something behind nagged at her. "Percival who?"

"The Realtor. I saw his sign on a tiny little storefront on Main Street yesterday. It's a sweet little shop. Used to be an antiques shop, until Lucy Higgins retired and moved to Florida."

"I remember her. She gave me a lace handkerchief once. Told me every young lady needs a handkerchief."

"Well, her store is empty now." Aunt Mabel traced over the triangles that formed a starburst on the quilt's panels. "It's a really nice place, too. The kind of place that would make a great office for a party planner."

Jenna zipped her suitcase shut, then slid it onto the floor. It was a little lighter than when she'd first arrived, because her suits were now with Tammy, but still the Samsonite hit the floor with a soft thud. "Gee, is that a hint?"

Aunt Mabel shrugged. "Call it a suggestion."

"A pretty obvious one." Jenna laughed.

Aunt Mabel's light blue eyes met her niece's. "Don't you want to live to be a hundred?"

"What's that got to do with Lucy Higgins's store?"

"Lucy retired at eighty-five. You know why she kept that shop open as long as she did? Working long past the age most people retire?"

"Because she needed the money?"

"Because running that little shop made her happy. Didn't make her rich, but sure made her happy." Aunt Mabel rose. She cupped Jenna's jaw in the same tender way she had when Jenna had been a little girl. "What you're doing now isn't making you happy, my dear. You keep telling yourself it is, but I know you as well as I know my own self, and you are searching for something, something that you already have here."

Jenna opened her mouth to argue back. The sentences formed on her tongue, but refused to leave her mouth.

Aunt Mabel was right. Jenna had been telling herself

that once her business was back on track, she'd be happy. She'd find that missing ingredient that had been plaguing her for months, no, years. But she hadn't, even as she'd stood in the middle of Eunice Dresden's birthday party, surrounded by happy, content guests.

She had, however, felt that sense of satisfaction earlier today. When she'd stood in the basement of the church and promised to help Father Michael plan the shelter's fundraiser.

"Running a business like that out of a town this small would be tough," Jenna said. "I mean, I'm sure I'd draw a lot from nearby cities, like Indianapolis, but still, it would take time to spread the word."

Aunt Mabel smiled. "Good thing you have a whole town to rally behind you. Who better to spread the word than your friends and neighbors?"

Jenna thought of what Earl had said, and what people like Father Michael and Betsy had done, and what they were still doing to help the people of the community. Riverbend truly was a family, complete with the quirky uncles and overbearing aunts.

The kind of family that had always been here, waiting for her. She'd let what a couple of people said ruin this town for her. No more. She realized what had bothered her all these days about going back to New York—

Her heart wasn't in the big city. It never had been. It had always been right here, in Riverbend's center.

"Friends and neighbors," Jenna repeated softly, then hefted the suitcase back onto the bed, unzipped it and began to unload everything she had just put inside. While Aunt Mabel stood beside her and cried.

Stockton had been a fool.

He stared at the ring box sitting on his dresser and

wondered how it was possible for a man to make the same mistake twice in one lifetime. He'd woken up this morning, and for a second he'd thought it was the day of Eunice's birthday party again. That he had a second chance to make things right between himself and Jenna. Then he saw the ring box and realized that day had already passed.

His cell phone rang. Stockton yanked it up, flipped it open and barked a greeting. "Yeah?"

"Yo, Stockton, this is Larry. You sick or something? Everyone's here waiting for you, for the staff meeting."

Stockton glanced at his watch and let out a low curse. In the year Rustica had been open, he had never been late. Never called in sick. And here he was, daydreaming and running a half hour behind. "I'll be right—" His gaze lighted on the ring box again. He thought of Jenna's words yesterday, accusing him of using his business as a way to avoid his fears. To avoid going after what he really wanted. To avoid committing to another person.

Damn. She was right. He *had* done that for the past two weeks—always, coming back to work instead of going after the thing he wanted most in life. Only a fool would keep doing something that wasn't working, and sure as hell wasn't making him happy.

"I'm, uh, not coming in today."

"You're…what?" Larry sputtered. "I think we have a bad connection because I thought I just heard you say you're not coming in today."

"You can handle the meeting and service today, Larry. I've got some…personal things to take care of." Larry spouted a few more objections, but Stockton cut him off. "You'll be fine. I'll see you tomorrow." Then he hung up the phone, grabbed his jacket and headed out the door.

* * *

Aunt Mabel had swept the front parlor twice already. Mopped the kitchen before the sun finished rising, and had fluffed the pillows on the parlor loveseat so many times, Jenna was surprised there was any pouf left in them. "Aunt Mabel, what are you doing?"

"Preparing for the first footer. A few days late, I might point out, but better late than never." She grabbed a dust rag and a bottle of furniture polish and set to work on the bookshelves.

"The first...what?" Jenna took the rag from her aunt's hands. "Here, let me do that."

"Goodness gracious, Jenna. I swear you never pay attention." Aunt Mabel handed over the cleaning products, then faced her niece. "The first footer is the first visitor of the new year."

"Aunt Mabel, the new year is already almost a week old. Surely—"

"We haven't had any visitors since the clock struck midnight on New Year's Eve. But we will today." She smiled, then fluffed the pillows. Again.

Jenna sighed and finished dusting. There was no arguing with her aunt when it came to her superstitions. Most days, they were just a funny quirk, but every once in a while, they drove Jenna crazy.

"You know the rules about first footers, don't you?" Aunt Mabel asked when Jenna finished the bookcase.

"Uh, no, not particularly. And really, I think—"

"In order to have good luck for the year, the first footer must be a man. Preferably a dark-haired man." Aunt Mabel grinned. "And he can't be cross-eyed or flat-footed. Both of those are bad signs."

Jenna laughed. "Well, I think you just crossed poor Earl off your list. That man's got the flattest feet in Indiana."

Aunt Mabel gave her niece a gentle swat. "Earl is not

coming to visit today. At least," she put a finger to her lips, "I don't think he is."

"How do you know anyone at all is coming by?"

"I dropped the tea towel this morning when I was making my coffee. It fell clear on the floor, right past my fingertips." Aunt Mabel wagged a finger. "That, my dear, is a sure sign a visitor is on his or her way."

Jenna shook her head, but didn't argue the point. Aunt Mabel almost always had someone stopping by for tea, so the tea towel theory could apply to about any day of the week. "I have to run out for a little while. I have a meeting with Percival over at the shop." She held up a hand. "I'm not making any promises, Aunt Mabel. I'm just going to check it out as a possible location." If her memories of the little antiques store were right, though, the shop would make an excellent location for an event planning business, particularly one that focused on philanthropic events. It was long and narrow, with two wide plate glass windows at the front. Great visibility, and plenty of room for small tables and displays.

"I'm glad you decided to stay in Riverbend," Aunt Mabel said.

"I am, too." Jenna sighed.

Aunt Mabel reached for her niece, her voice and her touch gentle, filled with concern. "You're thinking about Stockton, aren't you?"

"I have to go," she said, instead of dealing with a subject that would bring her nothing but heartbreak. She'd half expected him to come running after her when she'd left Eunice's party last night, but no, he had let her go. Again. Her heart wrenched at the memory, but she told herself it was all for the best. What best she couldn't quite see right now.

"If you're going to live in this town, you're going to see

him," Aunt Mabel said. "Maybe every day. So why don't you just go talk to him this morning and see where the two of you stand?"

Jenna laughed. "If you had your way, Aunt Mabel, the preacher would be standing in the front parlor by the end of the day."

Aunt Mabel arched a brow and grinned.

Jenna wagged a finger at her. "Don't get any ideas."

"Well, goodness gracious, somebody better get some ideas. Lord knows the two of you are moving slow as snails."

Those words made her think of their time on the ice, the push-pull of their attraction as they circled the ice. And that kiss…

No matter what happened, she was never going to forget that kiss. Or the one on New Year's Eve. Or any of the hundreds of times he'd touched her. That was going to be the hardest part about seeing Stockton from here on out—knowing what it was like to be with him, and knowing she never would again.

Stockton nearly tripped running up the stairs to Aunt Mabel's house. Had Jenna said her flight was last night? Or this morning? Damn, his brain was a muddled mess. He leaned hard on the doorbell.

The front door opened, sending a gust of warm air out into the winter chill. "Well, well, if it isn't Stockton Grisham." Aunt Mabel smiled. "Young man, you are as foolish as a squirrel trying to cross the highway. Come on inside, before you catch your death of a cold."

"I just want to know where Jenna is, Aunt Mabel."

"Nope, you have to come in to do that. Because you, Stockton, are the first footer." Aunt Mabel grinned and made a sweeping gesture of greeting. "The first guest to enter my house in the new year. And you are a man, and not flat-footed or cross-eyed."

He crossed the threshold and shot the older woman a curious glance. "The what?"

"First footer. A lucky omen, if you ask me." Aunt Mabel paused and tapped her chin. "Hmm...the only thing that would make this luckier would be if—"

"I brought a lump of coal with me?" Stockton held out his hand and dropped a shiny black rock into Aunt Mabel's palm.

Jenna's aunt beamed. "Exactly! A little coal to bring some warmth to the new year." She patted his cheek, then kissed his face. "Thank you, Stockton."

"Gee, Aunt Mabel, you wouldn't have tried to set that up by leaving that rock on the steps, would you?"

She grinned again. "Of course not. Well, maybe I nudged Lady Luck...a little."

"Maybe that's a good thing, because I think I need some luck today." He glanced into the house, up the stairs, down the hall to the kitchen. "I need to see Jenna. Is she here?"

"Oh, my, you just missed her. She's—"

But Stockton was already gone, racing back down the stairs and climbing into his car. As he put it into gear and navigated the downtown streets of Riverbend, he dialed the number for the local travel agency, run by one of the women in his mother's bible study. "Paula? It's Stockton Grisham. Listen, I need a ticket to New York—"

He stepped on the brakes. The Jeep screeched in protest. Was that...?

"When do you want to leave?" Paula asked.

A grin curved up Stockton's face. "I don't think I need to. Thanks, Paula." He tossed the phone to the side, parked the Jeep and climbed out. He crossed the street, ignoring the blare of someone's horn, and stopped outside the dark and closed shop that used to house an antiques store. "Jenna. You're still here. I thought you went to New York."

She pivoted toward him, a key in her hand. "I changed my mind."

His heart hammered in his chest. "Changed your mind?"

She held up the key and smiled. "It looks like Riverbend's population is going to grow by one more."

"You're...you're staying here?"

"I'm relocating my business here. And changing directions. From party planning to charitable events." She glanced back at the storefront and peace filled her features. "That's what I was missing all this time. A purpose to my work."

"I think that's the perfect combination for you."

"Me, too." Jenna's gaze traveled over the rows of businesses that lined Main Street. One of Aunt Mabel's neighbors came out of the corner bookstore. She raised a hand in greeting, and Jenna waved back. It was a small moment, the kind that happened every day in towns all across America, but it filled Jenna with a sense of belonging.

Something she hadn't even known she wanted until she had it.

"When you plan a party," she went on, "it's all over once the decorations are down. I wanted something that had more lasting power. Something that...made a difference. And when Father Michael started talking about the fundraiser for the shelter, I realized that was exactly the kind of business I wanted."

Stockton smiled, and her heart fluttered. "Good."

"Good that I'm staying in town or good that I'm starting a charitable events business?"

"Both." He took a step closer and the cold air that had hovered between them seemed to disappear.

As much as Jenna wanted to stay in this circle of her and Stockton forever, she realized she was torturing herself, standing here and talking to him, wishing he'd say something he was never going to say. "Well, I better get going. I have a meeting with Percival—"

"You're always trying to escape, Jenna Pearson, and I'm always trying to catch you." He reached out and put a hand on her arm. Even through the wool, she could feel the heat of his grip. "And I really want to catch you."

Her heart trilled, her pulse skipped, but still she held back from hoping. She couldn't let herself do that, and be let down again. Because she'd fallen for Stockton all over again, and fallen even harder the second time, because she knew what she had given up eight years ago and didn't want to do it again.

He took a step closer. She caught the woodsy notes of his cologne. She could live to be a thousand and she'd never forget that scent. Everything about Stockton Grisham was implanted in her memory and she held her breath as she waited for him to speak again.

"I was coming after you, Jenna," he said. "I should have done it last night, but instead I went back to the restaurant and worked. Doing exactly what you said I always do. Retreating into work, and avoiding relationships. It's what my father did, and I was too stupid to realize what it cost him. Until I almost made the same mistake."

Her breath was still caught in her chest, and her pulse thundered in her veins. "What…what mistake is that?"

"My father buried himself in his work. He used it as a way to distance himself from his family, his own son. He did it literally and figuratively by working as a traveling chef, until finally, my mother filed for divorce. And even when I saw him in Italy, I realized he wasn't any happier there than he had been here. You know why?"

Jenna shook her head.

"Because he didn't have this." Stockton placed a hand on Jenna's heart, then placed hers on his. She could feel the steady thump-thump of his heart beneath her palm. It was a comforting, steady sound. Something she could depend on, for a long time to come. "I let you get away once, Jenna, because I thought it was easier to stay uncommitted than to connect. You were right. I might be living here, but in my heart, I was still wandering, looking for something that I already had. You."

Stockton's words echoed in her head, and joy swelled inside her chest. His smile seemed to fill her, and she finally allowed hope to spring to life. "Really?"

He nodded. "Really and truly. I was on the phone, buying a ticket to New York, when I saw you outside the shop. I was going to find you, no matter where you were. I would have taken a spaceship, if necessary."

She looked at his handsome face, and knew there was more than one reason she hadn't gotten on that plane last night. "I stayed because…you were right. I have been afraid to change. Afraid to take a risk. Most of all, afraid to return to Riverbend." She gestured toward the town that she had grown to care about in a way she never had before, because she had finally seen past the few negative people and into the heart of the town. "It was easier to run than to trust."

"Trust that people would be there when you needed them."

She nodded, and tears sprang to her eyes. This time, she let them come, let them fall. Let Stockton see inside her heart. "That's what small towns are all about, aren't they? Community. It was what I was searching for, and I didn't even know I wanted or needed it, until I found it."

She shook her head. "All these months, I thought I was struggling in my business because I had lost my touch. For years, I had been too consumed with building the business to notice anything other than the bottom line. Then, after I hired Livia, I had more time. Time to think, look around me, and when I did, I felt unsettled. Like I had made a mistake. I kept thinking if I moved to another apartment, or I landed another corporate account, everything would start to feel right. But it never did. It took coming here for me to realize that was because I left my heart…" She paused a moment and caught Stockton's deep blue gaze. "Right here."

"If you had left, you would have taken my heart with you. Which would have been an awful shame." He held her face in his hands, so gentle and sweet. "Because I love you, Jenna. I always have. I wish I'd been smart enough to tell you years ago."

He loved her. Not the silly infatuation love they'd had when they'd been in high school. Not the love between two lifelong friends. But the kind of love people built lives on. Started families with. Bought a house and lived a life with. "Oh, Stockton, I love you, too."

His smile lit his eyes. He reached up, whisked away her tears, and placed a gentle kiss on her cheek. "Ah, Jenna, you have no idea how long I've waited to hear you say you love me."

"As long as I've waited to hear you say it back," she whispered.

"Too long," he said softly, then drew back and the smile widened. "Well, after all that, I guess there's only one thing left to do."

She cocked her head. "One thing?"

He dropped to one knee and fished a box out of his

pocket. "Get married." He thumbed back the lid of the box, revealing the diamond ring inside.

Jenna gasped, and the tears that had stopped began anew. "Is that…my mother's ring?"

"Yes. And now, it's yours, thanks to your aunt Mabel." Stockton grinned. "Marry me, Jenna. Marry me because you love me. Marry me because you never want to say goodbye again. Marry me because—" he let out a sigh that touched the deepest places in her heart "—because I didn't know what I was giving up when you walked out of my life eight years ago, and now that I do, I'm damned grateful to have a second chance to get it back."

Marry him. Take that final step in trust and commitment, with Stockton Grisham. She could see it already—his hand in hers, the two of them standing at the end of the church aisle, promising to stay together forever. To settle down in this little town and build a life. And maybe someday, sit in a banquet hall surrounded by all their friends and family, celebrating decades together.

Her hand closed over the ring box, and with it, Stockton's fingers. "I told myself today that I could live in Riverbend, open up a business here and be happy for the rest of my life, but…I was wrong."

He swallowed hard. "Wrong?"

She nodded. The velvet of the box kissed against her fingertips, a waiting promise. "In my heart, I'm a small-town girl, after all. And a small-town girl can never be truly happy unless she marries the boy next door."

He grinned. "I lived two blocks away from you."

She drew him to her, and placed a soft, sweet kiss on his lips. "Close enough, Stockton Grisham. Close enough."

He was still kissing her as he slid the ring onto her finger. It nestled against her skin, as if it was always meant to be there. The same way she and Stockton fit together, like two pieces of a puzzle.

There was a sound behind them, of a car door shutting. Jenna and Stockton broke apart, and turned at the same time. Aunt Mabel stood on the sidewalk, beaming at them. "She said yes?"

Stockton nodded. "Guess I'll be calling you Aunt Mabel for real from here on out."

"Well, my goodness, it's about time. I was worried I'd be celebrating *my* hundredth birthday before you two got smart. So I came down here myself to make sure you did the right thing. And…goodness, you did." She drew both of them to her in a hug that nearly took Jenna's breath away. Then Aunt Mabel stepped back, and reached into the big front pocket of her long wool coat to withdraw a shiny U-shaped object. "To the new couple," she said, holding out what Jenna now saw was a horseshoe. "And always be sure the tines are pointing up, to hold in all that good luck."

Jenna's gaze met Stockton's. His blue eyes seemed to go on forever, like an ocean she would spend a lifetime exploring. "I don't think we're going to need the horseshoe, Aunt Mabel," she said, slipping her hand into Stockton's. He gave her fingers a squeeze, then wrapped his arm around her waist. "Because we're already lucky enough."

Stockton nodded. His fingers grazed over the diamond that promised a new beginning for both of them. "We found everything we wanted and needed, right here in Riverbend."

Jenna rose on her toes and pressed a kiss to Stockton's lips. "A new year, a new beginning—"

"For old loves who never forgot each other."

Jenna curved into Stockton's arms, and pressed her head to his chest. His heart beat steady, right in time with her own. "And never will."

Harlequin® *Romance*

Coming Next Month

Available February 8, 2011

BABIES AND BRIDES!

Wedding bells and the pitter-patter of tiny feet
can be heard in Harlequin® Romance this month
as we celebrate bouncing babies and radiant new brides!

REQUEST YOUR FREE BOOKS!
2 FREE NOVELS PLUS 2
FREE GIFTS!

HARLEQUIN *Romance.*

From the Heart, For the Heart

*Harlequin Romance author Donna Alward is loved
for her gorgeous rancher heroes.*

*Meet Wyatt as he's confronted by both a precious
little pink bundle left on his doorstep and his neighbor Elli
who's going to show him the ropes....*

Introducing
PROUD RANCHER, PRECIOUS BUNDLE

THE SQUAWKING QUIETED as Elli picked the baby up, and
Wyatt turned around, trying hard to ignore the feelings of
inadequacy as Darcy immediately stopped fussing.

"Maybe she's uncomfortable. What do you think, sweetheart?" Elli turned her conversation to the baby.

"What do you think is wrong?" Wyatt asked, putting the
coffee pot back on the burner.

A strange look passed over Elli's face, one that looked
like guilt and panic. But it was gone quickly. "I couldn't
say," she replied.

"But you were so good with her this afternoon." Wyatt
put his hands on his hips.

"Lucky, that's all. I just…remembered a few things."
The same strange look flitted over her features once more.

Wyatt took the coffee to the table. "You fooled me. You
looked like you knew exactly what you were doing." So
much so that Wyatt had felt completely inept. A feeling he
despised. He was used to being the one in control.

Elli and Darcy walked the length of the kitchen and
back. After a few moments, she admitted, "I haven't really
cared for a baby before. The things I thought of were simply
things I'd heard about. Not from experience, Mr. Black."

Her chin jutted up, closing the subject but making him

want to ask the questions now pulsing through his mind. But then he remembered the old saying—*Don't look a gift horse in the mouth.* He'd benefit from whatever insight she had and be glad of it.

"I don't really know what babies need," he said. "I fed her, patted her back like you did, walked her to sleep, but every time I put her down..."

Wyatt almost groaned. Of course. He'd forgotten one important thing. He'd been so focused on getting the formula the right temperature that he'd forgotten to check her diaper. Not that he had any clue what to do there either.

Pulling calves and shoveling out stalls was far less intimidating than one tiny newborn.

"She's probably due for a diaper change, isn't she." He tried to sound nonchalant. This was a perfect opportunity. Elli must know how to change a diaper. He could simply watch her so he'd know better for the next time.

Instead, Elli came around the corner of the counter and placed Darcy back in his arms. "Here you go, Uncle Wyatt," she said lightly. "You get diaper duty. I'll fix the coffee. Cream and sugar?"

Oh boy, Wyatt thought, looking down into Darcy's pursed face, his smug plan blown to smithereens. He was in for it now.

Will sparks fly between Elli and Wyatt?

Find out in
PROUD RANCHER, PRECIOUS BUNDLE
Available February 2011 from Harlequin Romance

Try these Healthy and Delicious Spring Rolls!

INGREDIENTS

2 packages rice-paper spring roll wrappers (20 wrappers)

1 cup grated carrot

¼ cup bean sprouts

1 cucumber, julienned

1 red bell pepper, without stem and seeds, julienned

4 green onions finely chopped— use only the green part

DIRECTIONS

1. Soak one rice-paper wrapper in a large bowl of hot water until softened.

2. Place a pinch each of carrots, sprouts, cucumber, bell pepper and green onion on the wrapper toward the bottom third of the rice paper.

3. Fold ends in and roll tightly to enclose filling.

4. Repeat with remaining wrappers. Chill before serving.

Find this and many more delectable recipes including the perfect dipping sauce in

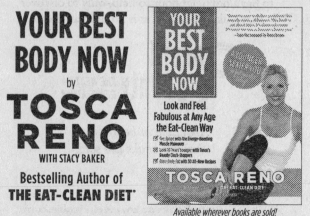

ROMANTIC SUSPENSE

Sparked by Danger, Fueled by Passion.

NEW YORK TIMES BESTSELLING AUTHOR

RACHEL LEE

No Ordinary Hero

Strange noises...a woman's mysterious disappearance and a killer on the loose who's too close for comfort.

With no where else to turn, Delia Carmody looks to her aloof neighbour to help, only to discover that Mike Windwalker is no ordinary hero.

Conard County *THE NEXT GENERATION*

Available in February.
Wherever books are sold.

SRS27709R2

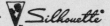

SPECIAL EDITION

FROM *USA TODAY* BESTSELLING AUTHOR

CHRISTINE RIMMER

COMES AN ALL-NEW BRAVO FAMILY TIES STORY.

Donovan McRae has experienced
the greatest loss a man can face, and
while he can't forgive himself, life—
and Abilene Bravo's love—are still
waiting for him. Can he find it in himself
to reach out and claim them?

Look for

DONOVAN'S CHILD
available February 2011